Mythical
Monsters

P9-EMO-674

Mythical Monsters

The Scariest creatures from legends, books, and movies

GENERAL EDITOR:
Chris McNab

tangerine Press
an imprint of
SCHOLASTIC
www.scholastic.com

Scholastic and Tangerine Press and associated logos are trademarks of Scholastic Inc.

Published by Tangerine Press, an imprint of Scholastic Inc.,
557 Broadway; New York, NY 10012

Scholastic Canada
Markham, Ontario

Scholastic Australia
Gosford NSW

Scholastic New Zealand
Greenmount, Auckland

Scholastic UK
Warwickshire, Coventry

Grolier International
Makati City, Philippines

10 9 8 7 6 5 4 3 2 1

ISBN-13: 978-0-439-85479-5
ISBN-10: 0-439-85479-2

Editorial and design by
Amber Books Ltd
Bradley's Close
74–77 White Lion Street
London N1 9PF
United Kingdom
www.amberbooks.co.uk

Project Editor: Sarah Uttridge
Design: Graham Curd

Printed in Singapore

CONTENTS

INTRODUCTION

Godzilla

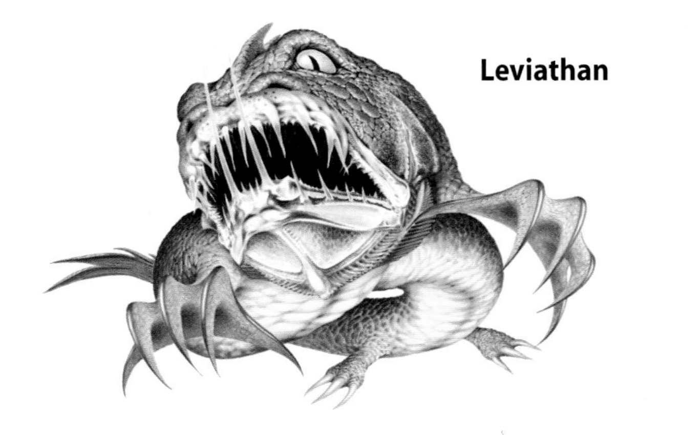

Leviathan

Dracula

For as long as humans have had fears, there have been stories about monsters. Some monsters were born of literature and myth—creatures such as Cyclops, the Sphinx, and the Basilisk. For ancient people, these were not mere fantasies, but real beliefs that haunted their lives. The citizens of Ancient Greece, for example, believed they faced an afterlife meeting with the three-headed dog Cerberus. In North America, Native Americans would tremble under the Thunderbird every time a storm slashed through the sky.

Legends of many ancient monsters often survived to terrorize people born hundreds of years later. The Basilisk, a lethal hybrid creature first described 2,000 years ago by the Roman writer Pliny, was still feared and encountered by the 16th century AD. In 1587, a Basilisk was said to have killed two young girls who were hiding in their cellar in Poland.

But haven't we moved on since then? Don't we know now that monsters are just products of fantasy? Don't be so sure. Several of the monsters in this book are certainly figures of pure invention. King Kong was created for cinema in 1933, and Godzilla has been a

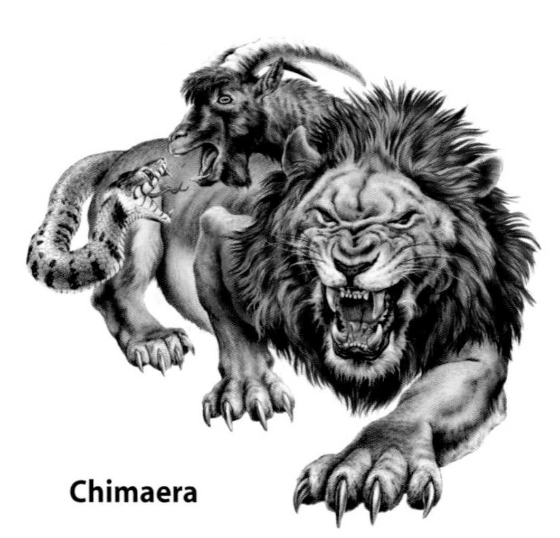

Chimaera

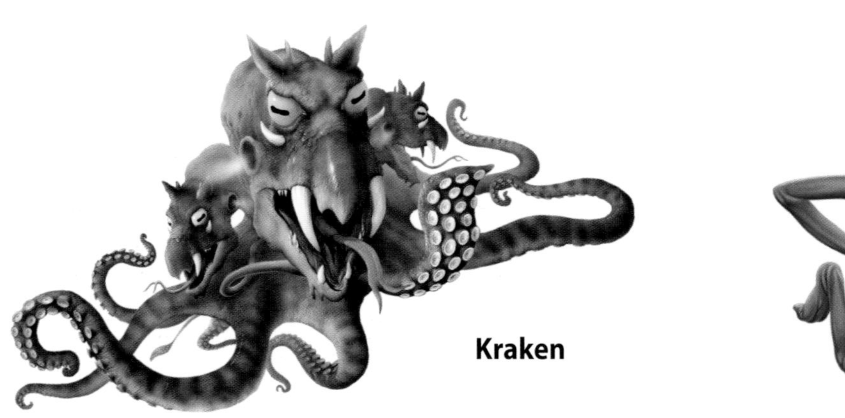

Kraken

Gray Alien

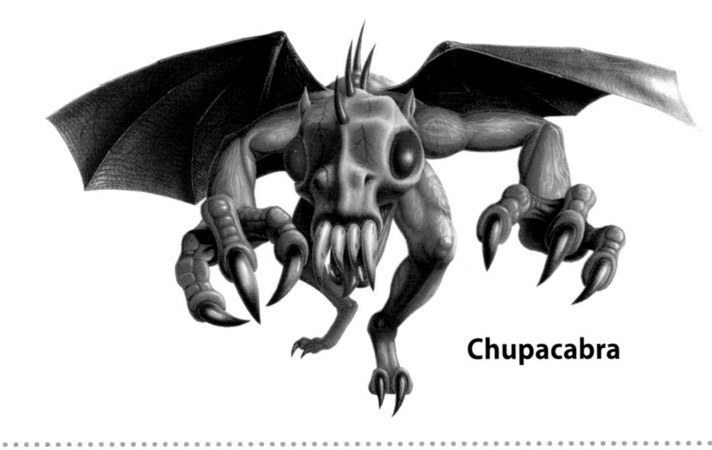

Chupacabra

Loch Ness Monster

Bigfoot

star of film and print for more than 50 years. Yet, countless witnesses throughout history have claimed that monsters are every bit as real as you or me—they have seen them with their own eyes! Thousands of people, for example, say they have been abducted by Gray Aliens. Scientists still aren't able to explain the huge footprints of the abominable snowman. More than 100 people claimed to see the blood-chilling Mothman around Point Pleasant, West Virginia, in 1966/67. And more than 1,000 people claimed to witness the Jersey Devil in 1909.

All such monster stories lurk somewhere between fantasy and reality. Everyone knows that some creatures are pure myth; but people love to hear a good story! Oftentimes, skeptics discredit modern monster stories by giving scientific explanations—like Bigfoot is just a big ape. But what's so wrong with believing? Thousands of witnesses can't all be lying, right? Don't let the skeptics fool you. It's human nature to be interested in the unknown, and many people—even the nonbelievers—secretly want to believe in these strange beasts.

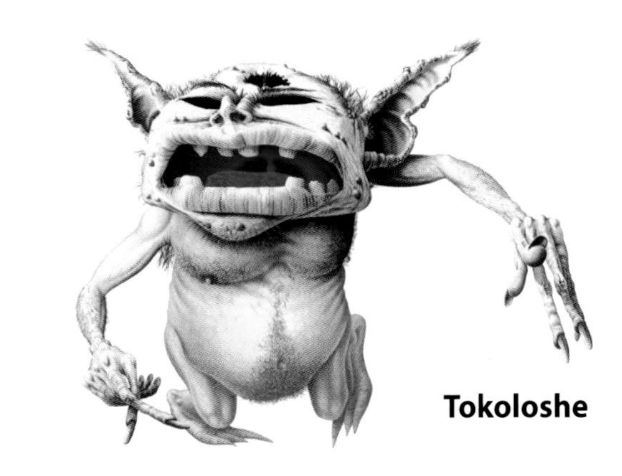

Tokoloshe

King Kong

Gorgon

BLACK DOG

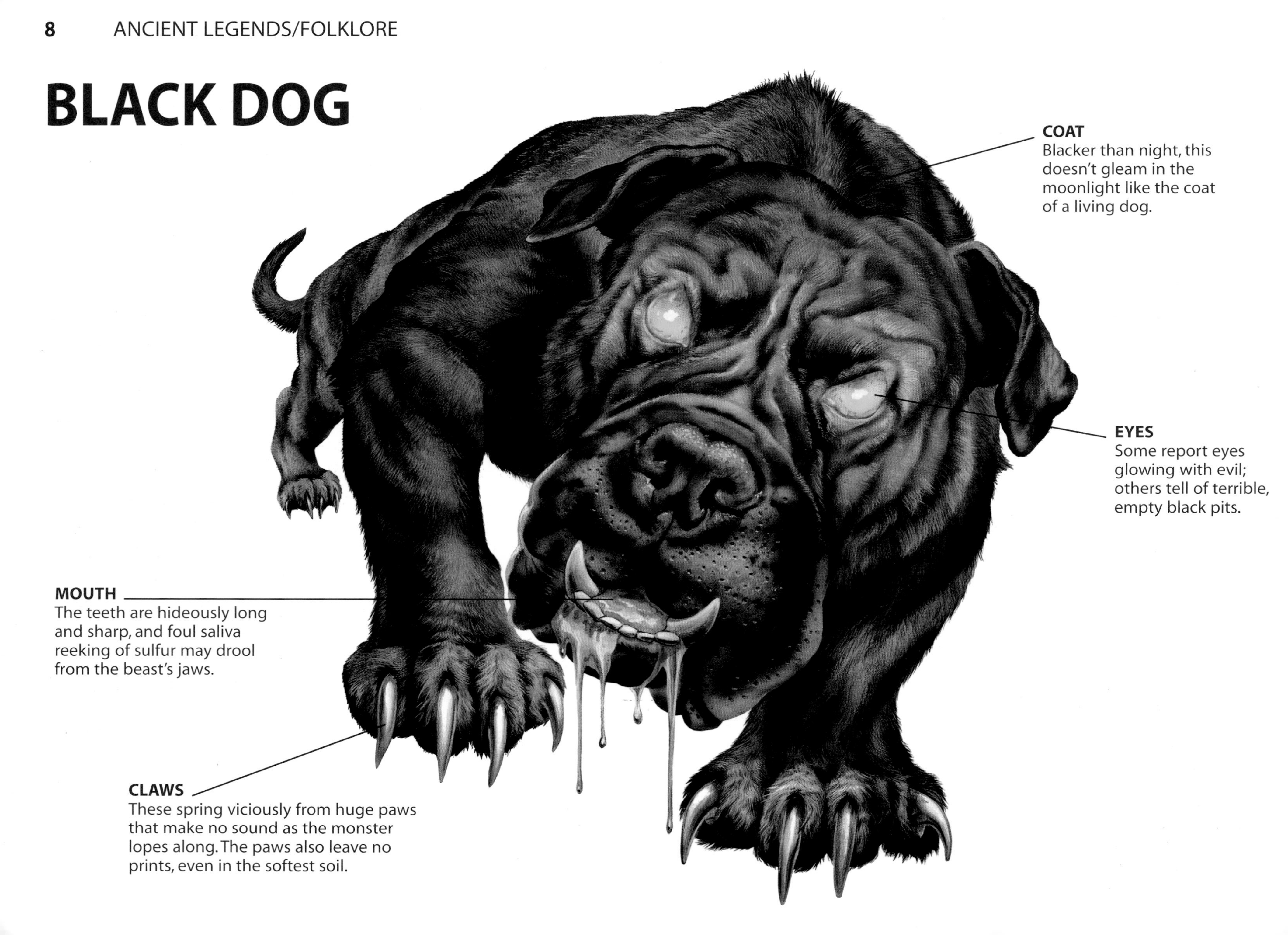
COAT
Blacker than night, this doesn't gleam in the moonlight like the coat of a living dog.
EYES
Some report eyes glowing with evil; others tell of terrible, empty black pits.
MOUTH
The teeth are hideously long and sharp, and foul saliva reeking of sulfur may drool from the beast's jaws.
CLAWS
These spring viciously from huge paws that make no sound as the monster lopes along. The paws also leave no prints, even in the softest soil.

A man walking home one evening takes a shortcut along a clifftop path. He doesn't believe local stories about a black dog. As he walks, a mist descends and he starts to feel cold—unnaturally so. Though uneasy, he presses on. Suddenly, he comes face-to-face with a monstrous, ghostly hound, its eyes burning with an unearthly fire. The man turns and runs in blind panic—and plunges over the cliff, clutching vainly at a tussock of grass as he falls screaming to his death.

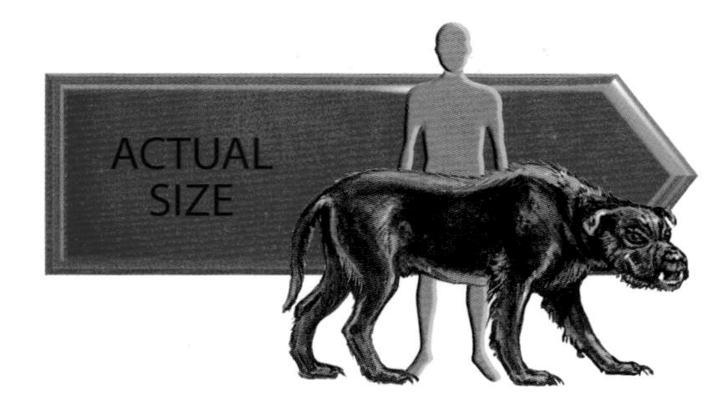

Folklore has it that if you see a phantom hound with a black coat and blazing eyes at night, bad luck or even death is close at hand. This huge dog has demonic red eyes, and it appears only at night, terrifying lone travelers. It is said that you will feel an unnatural chill before you see it appear. Tales of black dogs are especially rife in Britain, though some experts think Viking raiders brought these stories with them from Scandinavia. The dogs are often linked with churches. A black dog that visited the church of Blythburgh in Suffolk in 1577 killed three people. Black dog stories influenced Arthur Conan Doyle when he wrote his Sherlock Holmes story, *The Hound of the Baskervilles*.

WHERE IN THE WORLD?

Most tales of black dogs come from Britain and Ireland, but there have been sporadic sightings in Scandinavia, Germany, France and even as far afield as Nova Scotia in Canada and the eastern states of the USA.

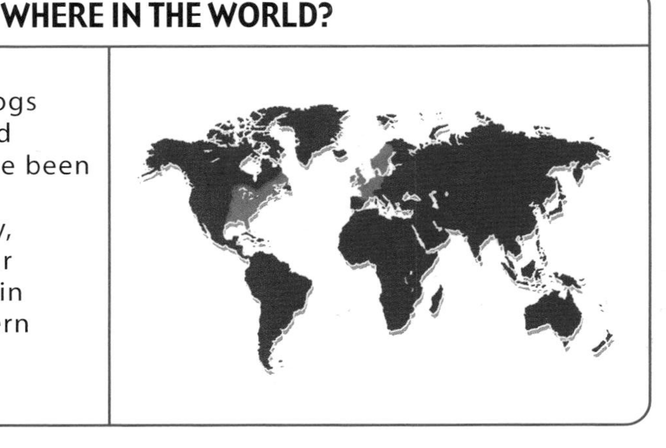

DID YOU KNOW?

- The earliest known report of a black dog was in France in AD 856, when one materialized in a church even though the doors were shut. The church grew dark as it padded up and down the aisle, as if looking for someone. The dog then vanished as suddenly as it had appeared.
- In Missouri in the USA, a hunter once threw an ax at an enormous black dog. The ax passed right through the beast's ghostly body.

BOGEYMAN

EYES
Large, dark and bulbous, the bogeyman's eyes are adapted to coping with the low light levels found under the bed and inside bedroom cupboards.

NOSE
This is wide and fat, ideal for sniffing out young victims.

FINGERNAILS
Long and terrifyingly sharp, these weapons rip through bedclothes to reach petrified victims cowering underneath.

SKIN
The bogeyman's skin is covered in warts and boils and he is keen to pass them on. If you've got a wart, the bogeyman might have paid you a visit.

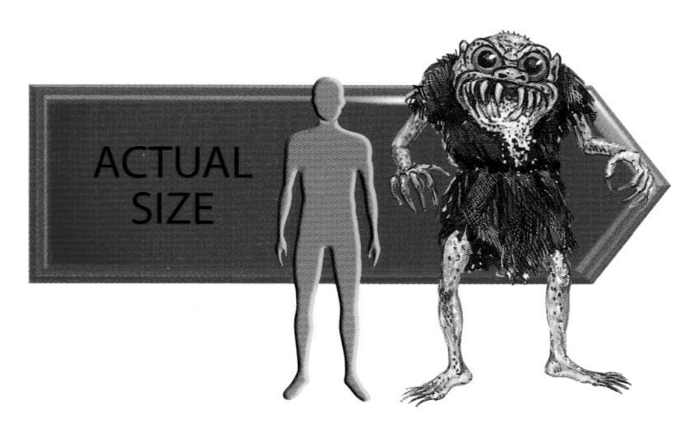

Once you switch off the bedroom light at night, your room suddenly turns into an unfamiliar place of strange shapes and eerie sounds. This is the domain of the bogeyman. One of the most common and widely feared monsters of North America, he's most likely to appear when you're in bed asleep. Angry parents sometimes threaten their children with a visit from this ogre.

A young boy lies in bed, too frightened to move as moonlight streaks through the curtains and throws eerie shadows across his blankets. His big brother had warned him that the bogeyman would get him if he was naughty. He had seen his brother dressing up as a monster for a Halloween party, and so he expects to get a scary visit. Then, out of the corner of his eye, he notices a shadowy form taking shape in the light streaming from a widening gap in the doorway. The door opens fully and there appears a gigantic form silhouetted against the light. Convinced that his brother is playing a trick, the boy throws back the covers and leaps on to the bed to confront him. "Stop it! It's not funny", the boy screams. But, relentlessly, the figure shuffles closer. As the mysterious form looms over his bed, the boy begins to wonder if it really is his brother after all…

WHERE IN THE WORLD?

The bogeyman is found mainly in North America, where many towns and districts have their own legends about this horrible being. Bogeyman tales are also told in the UK, especially in Scotland where stories of "bogeys" abound.

DID YOU KNOW?

- American communities often give the bogeyman local names such as "The Shape," "Rawhead Rex," and "The Hook."
- The word "bogeyman" may have come from Scotland, where mischievous goblins are called bogles, bogeys and boggarts.
- There is a bogeywoman who haunts the midwestern USA, where she scratches on bedroom windows to scare small children. England also has a bogeywoman tale. Jenny Greenteeth haunts the county of Lancashire UK, where she preys on children who play too close to streams and ponds. Green slime on the water's surface is taken as a sign of her presence.

CHUPACABRA

SPINES
These reportedly burst through the skin of the monster's head and back. Their purpose is unknown, but they may offer protection against enemies.

SIZE
Eyewitness accounts are muddled. Estimates of the creature's height in the standing position vary from 3ft 3in (1m) to 6ft 6in (2m) .

WINGS
The chupacabra is usually said to have bat-like wings with a span up to 13ft (4m). A few reports say it has no wings.

EYES
The size of hens' eggs, the big eyes glow an alien red. Some witnesses claim they fire laser beams to paralyze victims!

CLAWS
The monster's feet and hands have huge, viciously curved and wickedly sharp claws for pinning down helpless prey.

LEGS
These are long and muscular for bounding 66ft (20m) at a stride when advancing on prey. Strangely, the monster never leaves footprints.

FANGS
Witnesses say the chupacabra's mouth bristles with great fangs. Some say they are bright red.

SKIN
Some witnesses say the beast has bare gray or blue skin, others that it has scales or fur.

A chupacabra swoops toward a small herd of goats and drops silently between the trees —a ragged silhouette against the night sky. Sensing danger, the goats shuffle nervously, then start to bleat in panic as the monster strides toward them, moving unnaturally fast on its long legs. Paralyzed by terror and the foul, sulfurous odor of the chupacabra, the goats are helpless to flee. The monster seizes the nearest one with its claws, plunges its huge fangs into the animal, and swiftly sucks out every last drop of blood. Goat after goat, it drains the whole herd, then slips off in search of other prey—for a chupacabra's craving for blood is never satisfied. It leaves no tracks behind.

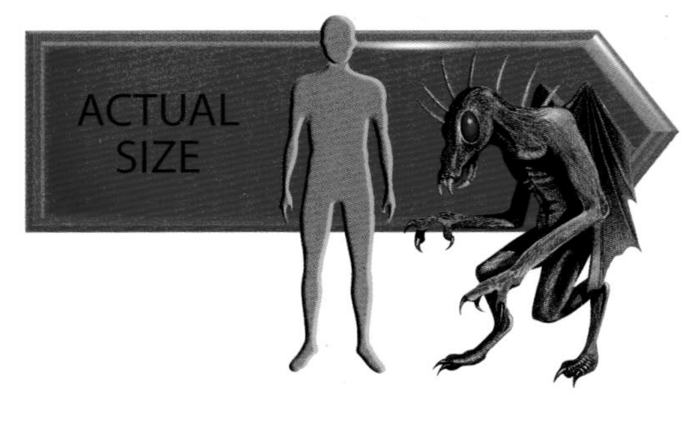

A modern menace of the Americas, this blood-sucking, bat-like fiend is blamed by farmers and the authorities alike for the brutal slaughter of pets and livestock. This multi-fanged, many-spined, foul-smelling monster was first reported in 1995. It seeks out its victims in the dark of night and preys on a range of farm and domestic animals, sucking them dry of blood – its name means "goat-sucker," after its first victim. Some people say that the chupacabra comes from outer space, while others say it is the result of US military experiments.

WHERE IN THE WORLD?

The chupacabra is known in Central and South America. There are also reports from the southern states of the USA, including California, Arizona, Texas and Florida. Most sightings are from Puerto Rico, an island 994 miles (1600km) southeast of Florida.

Puerto Rico

DID YOU KNOW?

- Two Brazilian fishermen claim they shot a chupacabra dead and still have its head—which they refuse to let anyone examine.
- The mayor of Canovanas, a town in Puerto Rico, leads chupacabra search parties, armed with a crucifix and a gun. He also sets traps around the town in the hope of catching one of the elusive creatures.
- In 1996, a Mexican policeman opened fire on a chupacabra at close range—but his bullets had no effect, and the monster escaped.
- Attacks on humans are rare, but a nurse in Mexico reportedly lost an arm to the fangs of a chupacabra.

GOGMAGOG

HEAD
Wild-haired, slack-mouthed and piggy-eyed, Gogmagog was incredibly ugly by human standards.
STATURE
Gogmagog stood almost 13ft (4m) tall, and was so strong he could rip up trees by the roots.
BODY
Clothed in roughly stitched animal skins, the giant's body bulged with muscle.
WEAPONS
Sometimes the giant brandished a cudgel, and sometimes he fought with a huge battle-ax or a spiked ball-and-chain.
FEET
The entire ground shook as Gogmagog stomped around on his huge feet.

Gogmagog was one of the last of the mighty giants of Albion: a demonic race of fiercely aggressive beings who lived on the island that later became Britain. The giants were spawned by one of the exiled daughters of the Roman Emperor Diocletian and a demon. Despite their great power, they were soon threatened by a Trojan invasion. The giants vigorously resisted the Trojan soldiers and initially drove them back, but their army was defeated after the invaders dug hidden trenches full of stakes. The giants killed many Trojan warriors, but succumbed to their superior fighting skills until, finally, only Gogmagog was left alive. He too was finally killed by the Trojan warrior Corineus.

Only 20 giants escape the Trojans' deadly traps, including Gogmagog, the strongest of them all. He waits until the invaders are celebrating a day dedicated to the gods, then leads the others in a frenzied attack. The rampaging giants tear many Trojans limb to limb, while Gogmagog simply picks them up and kills them in one blow. But Brutus and Corineus rally their men and, one by one, the giants are overwhelmed.

WHERE IN THE WORLD?

According to legend, the Trojans landed in Albion (Britain) at the site of either modern Totnes or modern Southampton. Gogmagog met his fate in the sea close to Totnes, where a cliff still bears the name Lan-Goenagog, or Giant's Leap.

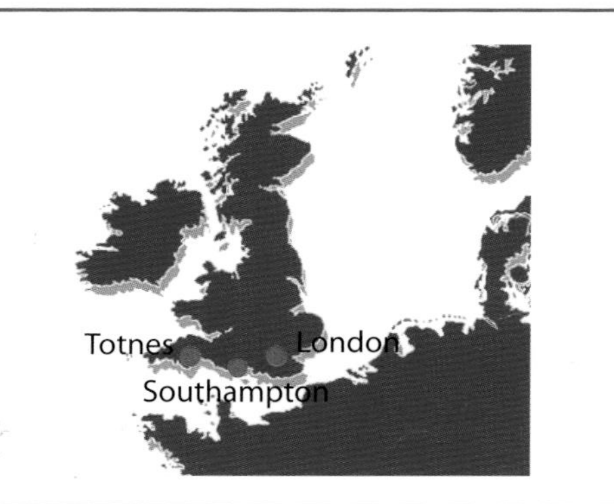

DID YOU KNOW?

- In legend the warrior Brutus renamed Albion "Britain" after himself, and after receiving the west of the country as his share, the warrior Corineus called it "Cornwall."
- Many associate the names Gog and Magog to the hostile forces of Satan, which are due to appear just before the end of the world.
- Tales of giants may have been inspired by huge prehistoric figures cut into the chalk hills of Britain.

GOLEM

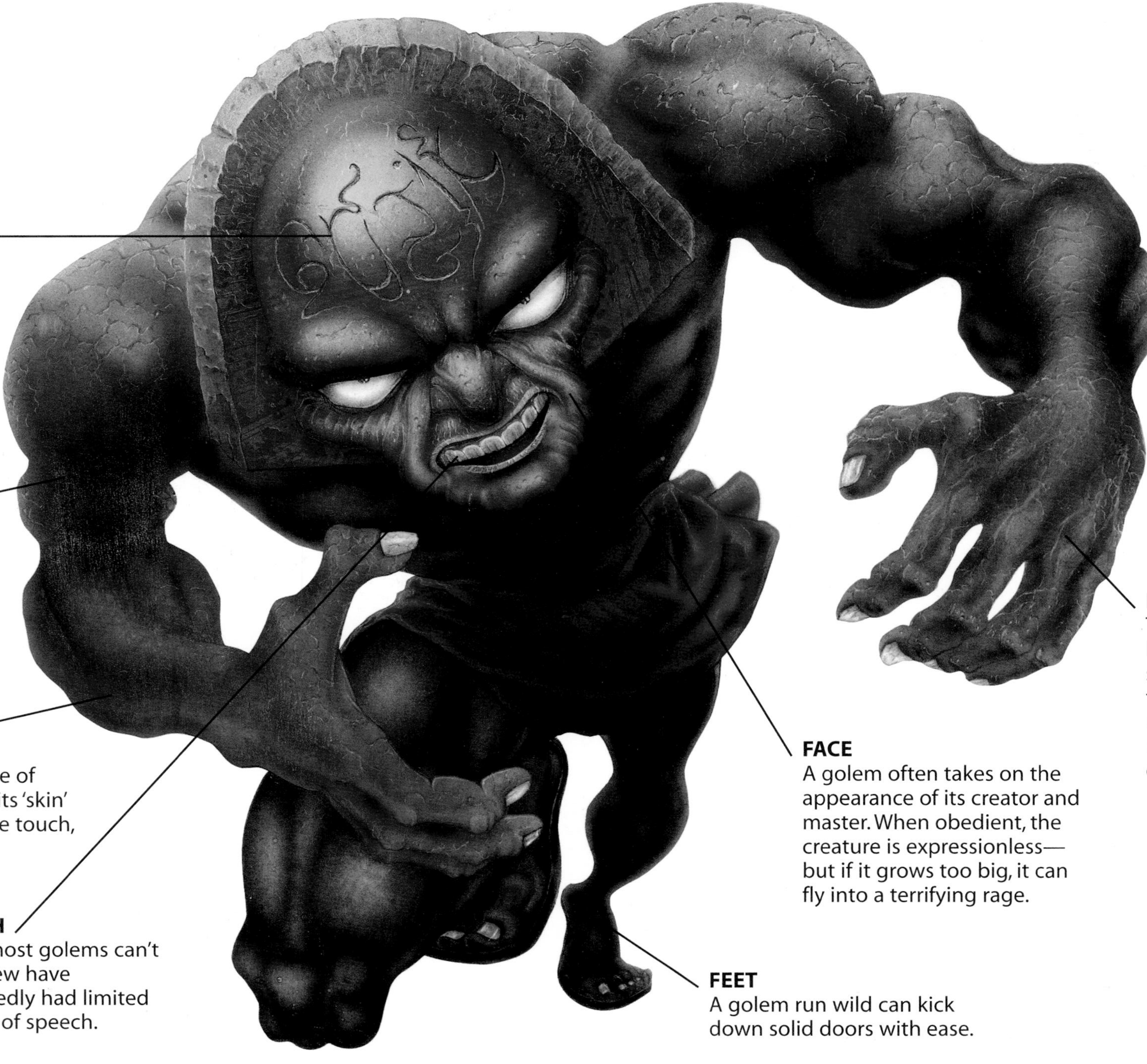

FOREHEAD
One way to bring a golem to life is to write a special word on its forehead. Erasing the word is then the only way to kill the monster.

MUSCLES
If allowed, a golem can grow immensely strong. When it is on one of its rampages, it can hurl boulders around as if they were pebbles.

SKIN
A golem is usually made of clay, stone or wood, so its 'skin' is hard and rough to the touch, and extremely tough.

MOUTH
While most golems can't talk, a few have supposedly had limited powers of speech.

FACE
A golem often takes on the appearance of its creator and master. When obedient, the creature is expressionless—but if it grows too big, it can fly into a terrifying rage.

HANDS
These grow bigger and stronger all the time and are a rampant golem's main tools of destruction.

FEET
A golem run wild can kick down solid doors with ease.

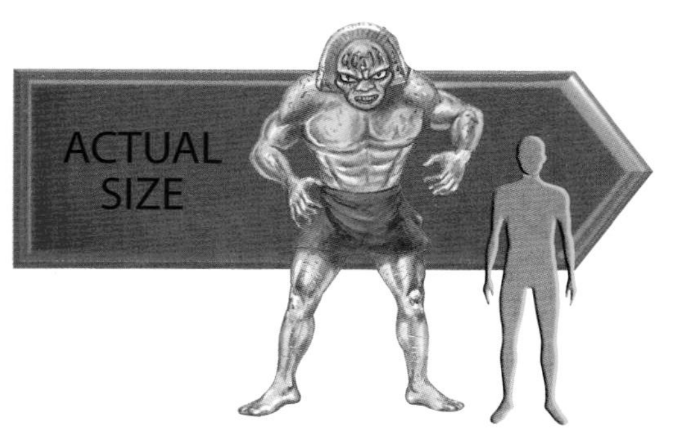

A golem is one of mythology's more unusual creatures. It is a figure made from clay, wood or stone, and then brought to life by its creator. Once living, the golem then acts as a guardian and protector over its creator, and it obeys its master's every command. Ominously, the golem also grows bigger and stronger every day. Here is the danger. If the golem becomes too large, it can become wild and destructive. The creator must destroy and rebuild it before it becomes out of control and a danger to everyone.

An absent-minded golem-maker has neglected to destroy his creation, and the beast has grown so huge and monstrous that it is now ransacking its master's house. The devastation may not end here, though, for if no-one can reach up to erase the magical, life-giving word from the creature's forehead, it may end up obliterating everything—and everybody—in its path.

WHERE IN THE WORLD?

Historically, golems have most often been made in Eastern Europe, but a golem can be created from such a range of widely abundant and easily available materials that a sorcerer can make one almost anywhere in the world, at any time.

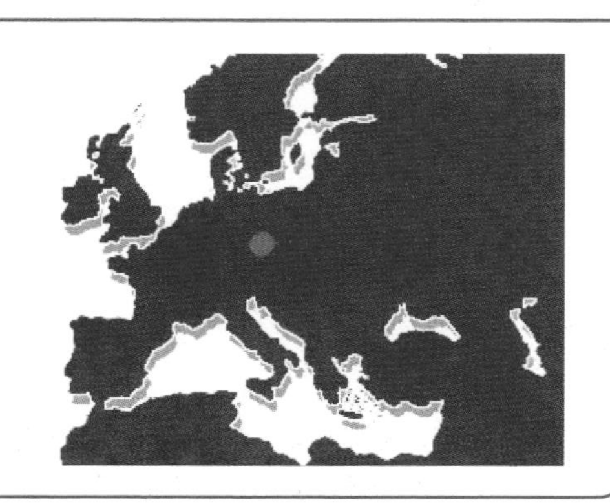

DID YOU KNOW?

- Tibetans have their own golem, a tulpa, which obeys orders but can develop a personality of its own.
- Vietnamese sorcerers called the Thay Phap make human puppets out of wood or straw, breathe life into them and order them to rob and kill.
- In Spain in the 11th century, the philosopher Solomon ibn Gabirol was acquitted of sorcery after he agreed to destroy his female Golem.

LEVIATHAN

SCALES
Tougher than the stoutest shield and tightly overlapping, these form an impenetrable armor that makes the monster invulnerable to human weapons such as swords, spears and harpoons.

JAWS
No one escapes the gaping jaws, which are lined with rows of terrible teeth and belch out sparks and flames.

FINS
Spiny pectoral fins easily slice flesh from bone, but also come in handy when the monster wants to drag his massive body onto rocks.

BODY
Long and immensely powerful, the serpentine body coils and writhes as Leviathan surges through the water, creating a frothing, white wake behind him.

CHEST
Leviathan's powerful neck and chest bulge with sinews like great ropes of iron, and within his chest beats a cold, unfeeling heart as hard as stone.

Stirring up the ocean with his mighty tail, Leviathan creates a seething wall of water that gathers speed, bursts over the shore and completely overwhelms a small fishing village. Huts are shattered like matchwood and screaming victims are swept out to their deaths. A few locals escape the carnage by climbing trees, and they can only watch in horror as the monster rears out of the water to gloat at his handiwork and gobble up anyone washed out to sea.

This primeval sea monster dominates the watery wastes of the world and has power over all the creatures of the ocean. He is chaos and evil personified, and he brings death and disaster in his foaming wake. His body stinks like a rotten carcass and he drinks the entire flow of rivers every day. His furnace-hot breath makes the sea boil, and when he sneezes, smoke billows from his nose. The Leviathan is first mentioned in Middle Eastern creation myths dating back more than 5000 years ago. According to Hebrew texts, Yahweh (God) made Leviathan and a female mate on the fifth day of Creation, but promptly killed the female to stop her producing offspring that might destabilize the world.

WHERE IN THE WORLD?

Leviathan has his origins in early Hebrew writings from the Middle East, dating back to about 3000 years BC. The Hebrews occupied Turkey, Syria, Jordan, Israel, Iraq and Iran—but the monster has the run of all the world's oceans.

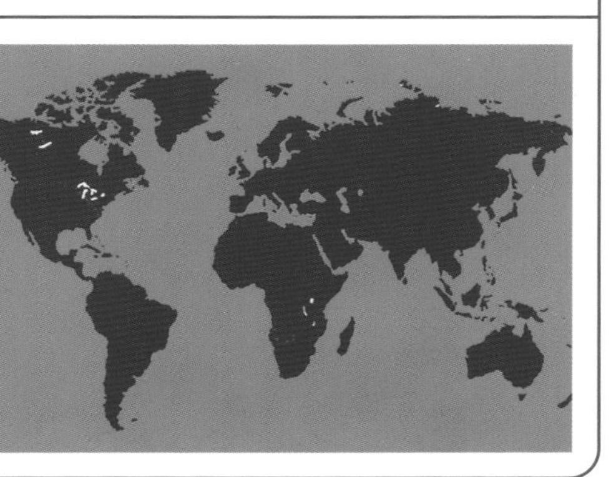

DID YOU KNOW?

- Early images of Leviathan from seal-stones and weapons show the monster with seven heads.
- Christians have identified Leviathan with Satan, with his huge mouth being the entrance to Hell.
- Most fish swim willingly into Leviathan's jaws, apart from the tiny stickleback. This he fears—for the stickleback was created to keep him in check.

MERPEOPLE

HAIR
These flowing locks are a mermaid's pride and joy. She spends many hours gazing in a silver mirror, combing through the lustrous strands.

SKIN
A mermaid's flawless skin seems pale and translucent in water, and may have a greenish tinge.

UPPER BODY
Above the waist a mermaid looks like a beautiful woman. She is very attractive, especially to lonely sailors.

LOWER BODY
Instead of legs, a mermaid sports a scaly tail like a fish, with a wide fin for powering through the water.

JEWELS
A mermaid is incredibly vain and often drapes herself with ropes of sea pearls and other stolen jewels.

A ship has been at sea for several months when the weary sailors find themselves caught in a sudden storm. As their vessel pitches and rolls, the men batten down the hatches and fight to keep their ship afloat, but soon they hear a haunting voice above the noise of the waves. Gradually, they forget their duties and crowd to the side of the deck, straining to hear the beautiful sound—and the ship drifts inexorably toward some jagged rocks. Catching sight of an alluring female form, the sailors cry out. They seem oblivious to the danger, until the ship hits the rocks with a savage lurch that jolts several of them overboard. Struggling uselessly against the pounding surf, the last thing each sailor hears before he drowns is the evil mermaid laughing delightedly as the ship is torn apart.

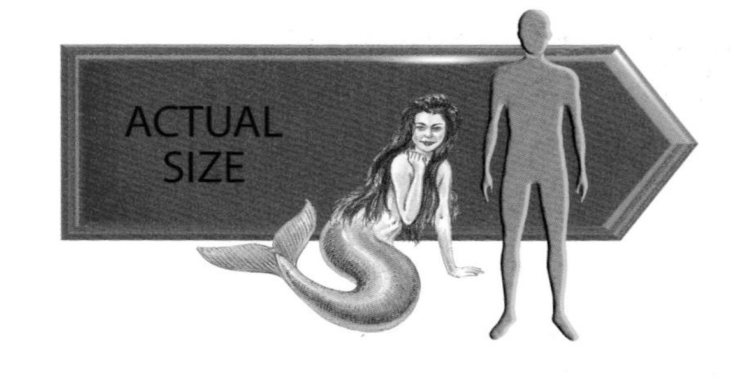

Merpeople are beautiful and elusive creatures, sometimes glimpsed lounging on coastal rocks or swimming through the ocean waves. The earliest stories of these semi-human sea creatures came from ancient Babylon (now in Iraq) about 7000 years ago. They can also spell disaster for those mariners who see them. Whenever they appear, storms, shipwrecks and drownings follow close behind. Mermaids, for example, tempt ships onto rocks by bewitching the sailors with their great beauty and haunting songs.

WHERE IN THE WORLD?

Merpeople live in all the world's oceans and seas. Sailors usually spot them lounging on rocks along the coast or frolicking out at sea, though a few venture inland by swimming up rivers.

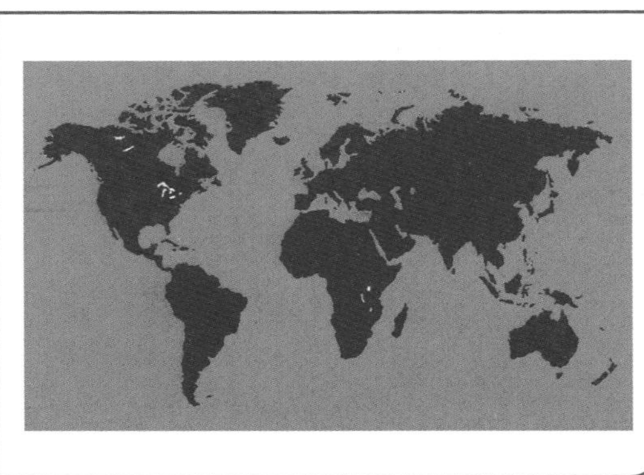

DID YOU KNOW?

- Merpeople are said to hoard vast treasure-troves of gold, jewels and other valuables, which they gather from the hulks of sunken wrecks.
- In the 6th century, legend says a mermaid visited a monk on the remote island of Iona, Scotland, asking for a soul. When the monk demanded that she leave the sea for good, the mermaid left the island crying. Her tears turned into gray-green pebbles that can still be found on the beaches.
- In 1961, the Isle of Man tourist board held a fishing competition where a prize was offered to anyone capturing a mermaid. No one claimed the prize, but there were many reported sightings.

MUMMY

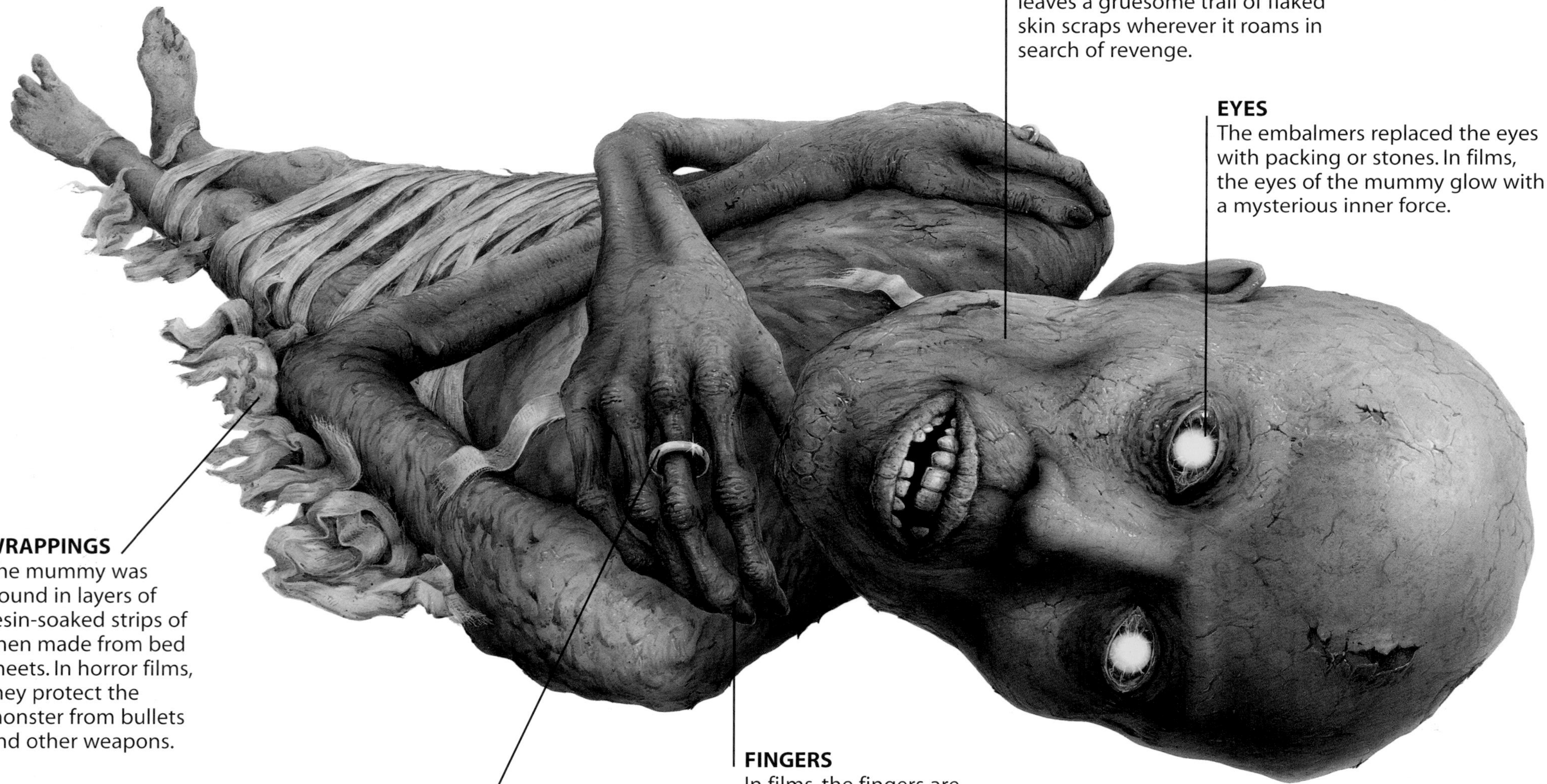

SKIN & LIPS
Embalming dried out the body completely, leaving skin, lips and other tissues cracked and shriveled. In films, the mummy leaves a gruesome trail of flaked skin scraps wherever it roams in search of revenge.

EYES
The embalmers replaced the eyes with packing or stones. In films, the eyes of the mummy glow with a mysterious inner force.

WRAPPINGS
The mummy was bound in layers of resin-soaked strips of linen made from bed sheets. In horror films, they protect the monster from bullets and other weapons.

MAGIC CHARMS
Charms such as magic rings gave the mummy great power.

FINGERS
In films, the fingers are long and powerful—ideal for throttling.

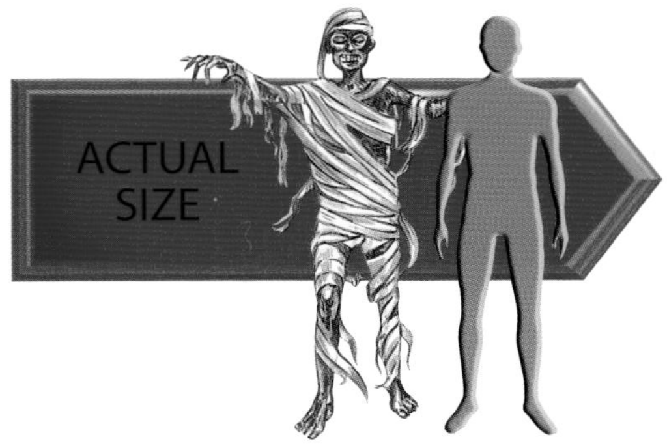

Ancient Egyptians carved grim threats on the tombs of their embalmed kings, warning the living not to disturb the grave—or risk the wrath of the mummy... The mummy is an embalmed body that has survived intact in its secret tomb for thousands of years. Wrapped in strips of linen and sealed away with gold, jewels and other treasure, it is protected by a curse. In horror films, the mummy comes to life to take revenge on robbers and archaeologists who dare to invade its tomb.

Two archaeologists and their hired workers have spent weeks hacking at the rocks, and now the tomb's entrance is revealed. Also visible are the symbols spelling out a dire threat. The workers grow restless, but the archaeologists dismiss their fears. Using heavy axes, the workers rain blows on the entrance, which shatters with a deafening crack. Holding his blazing torch high, the lead archaeologist enters the tomb, with his colleague close behind. He looks around in awe as the torch's light glints off precious objects decorated with gold and jewels. A movement catches his eye and he turns to see a massive stone coffin open and a huge mummy appear. The mummy lumbers toward him with outstretched arms. Paralyzed with fear, the archaeologist stands helpless as he feels the mummy's powerful hands grip his throat—and begin to squeeze.

WHERE IN THE WORLD?

The best-known tombs of mummies are in the Valley of the Kings, in Egypt. The mummy of Tutankhamen still lies in his tomb here, near to the ancient cities of Thebes and Luxor, close to the River Nile. Other tombs were at Abydos, 93 miles (150km) farther downriver.

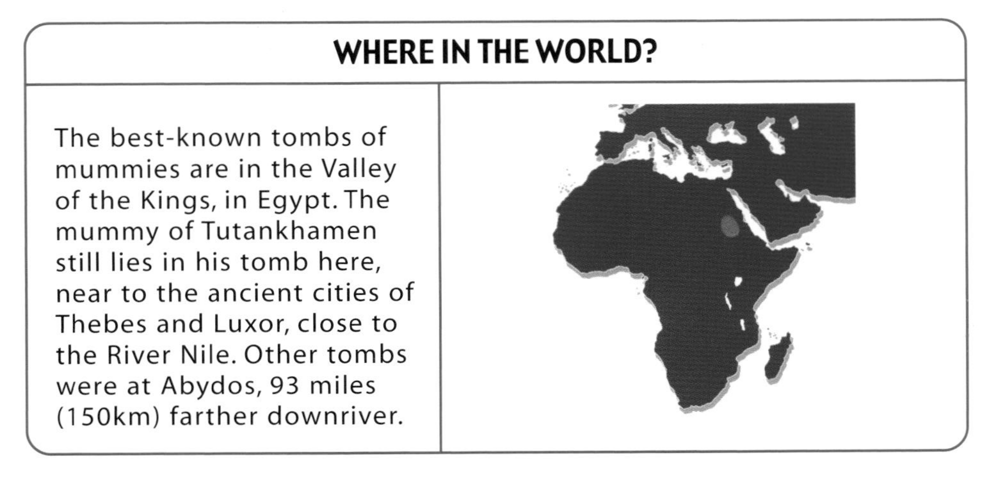

DID YOU KNOW?

- In medieval times, physicians often sold real or fake mummy's flesh and wrappings in powder form as a medicine. It was used to treat all disorders from acne to ulcers.
- Scientists set up the world's first international mummy tissue bank at Manchester Museum, UK, in the late 1990s. It holds tissue samples taken from mummies housed in museums around the world, for use in medical research.
- The Egyptian priests tried many different ways to protect the royal tombs, including inscribing bloodcurdling curses. They built huge granite doors and secret entrances.

TOKOLOSHE

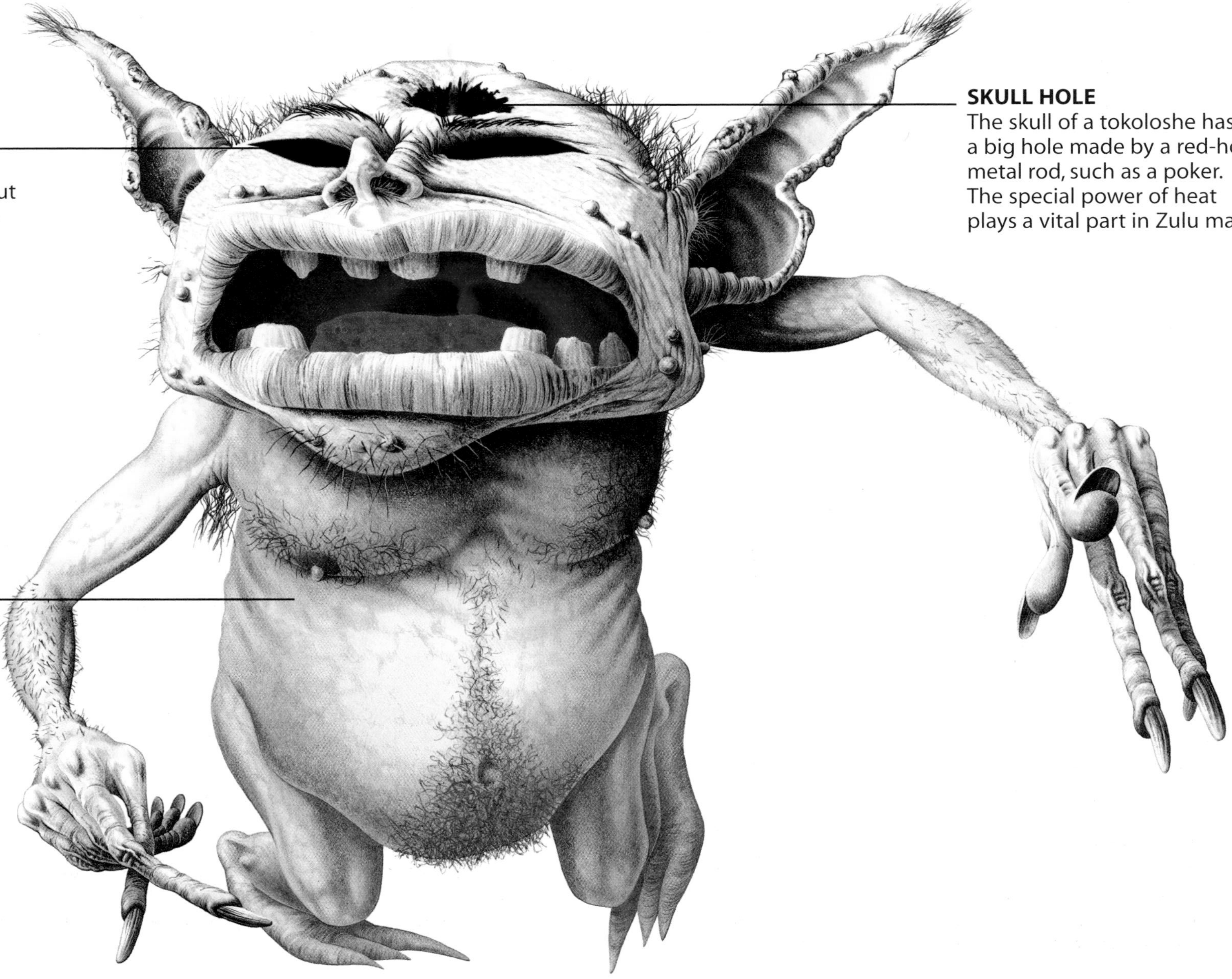

EYES
The eyes of a tokoloshe have been gouged out but it uses its other senses to find its way around.

SKULL HOLE
The skull of a tokoloshe has a big hole made by a red-hot metal rod, such as a poker. The special power of heat plays a vital part in Zulu magic.

BODY
Withered and gray, the body of a tokoloshe is far smaller than the corpse from which it was made.

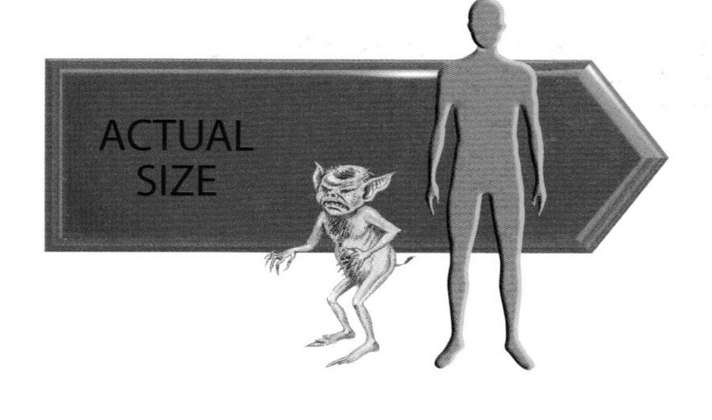

A woman has had an argument with a tribal elder and will pay the price. She arrives home to find a tokoloshe waiting. The diminutive creature leaps on the terrified victim, beating her with supernatural strength. The victim knows her bed is a haven from the horror. The bedstead is propped up on bricks that are wrapped in old paper, an ancient ploy against the fiend. The woman leaps onto the bedclothes, safe from attack but powerless to protect her home. The tokoloshe rampages through her home, smashing her possessions with demonic delight.

The tokoloshe is a twisted little creature. It lives in South Africa, and is a cross between a zombie, a poltergeist and a gremlin. Tokoloshes are created from dead bodies by *shamen*, or witch doctors, usually if the shaman has been offended by someone. Even though the tokoloshes are only the size of small children (the corpses shrivel up during the transformation), they can create terrible destruction. They attack people and property, often as the result of a curse. Worse still, only the person who is cursed will be able to see the tokoloshe—it is invisible to everyone else around. Once a tokoloshe is created, it will wander around causing mischief and mayhem.

WHERE IN THE WORLD?

Tokoloshes have been reported throughout southern Africa, but they are most active in Kwazulu/Natal, the Zulu province in western South Africa. However, no area is safe from the fiends. Once a tokoloshe has been created, no one can know for sure where it may turn up.

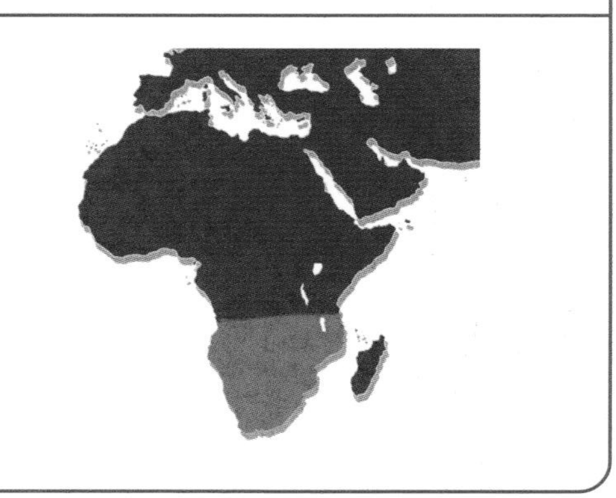

DID YOU KNOW?

- Tokoloshes have a strong dislike of schoolchildren and will often scribble on their schoolbooks or destroy their homework to get them into trouble with their teachers.
- Zulus usually blame misfortune on witchcraft. Suspected witches and their families are put to death and their property then given to the tribal chief.
- For some reason, wealthy villagers are far more likely to be accused of magic than poor people.

TROLL

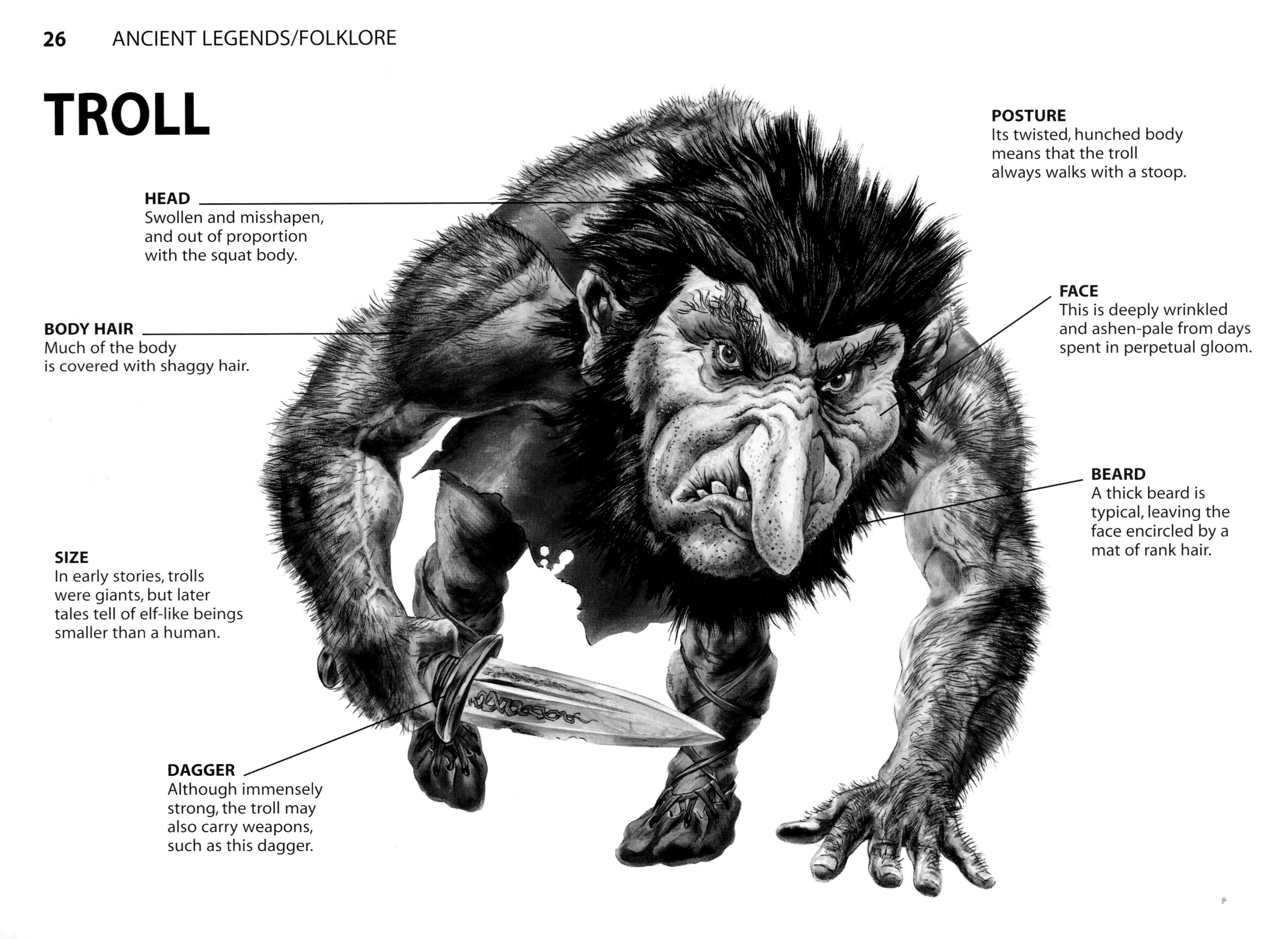
HEAD
Swollen and misshapen, and out of proportion with the squat body.
BODY HAIR
Much of the body is covered with shaggy hair.
SIZE
In early stories, trolls were giants, but later tales tell of elf-like beings smaller than a human.
DAGGER
Although immensely strong, the troll may also carry weapons, such as this dagger.
POSTURE
Its twisted, hunched body means that the troll always walks with a stoop.
FACE
This is deeply wrinkled and ashen-pale from days spent in perpetual gloom.
BEARD
A thick beard is typical, leaving the face encircled by a mat of rank hair.

A wicked troll is about to leave the scene of its nocturnal crime, holding a helpless human infant in its arms. The evil of the deed is two-fold, for not only has the troll stolen a baby, it has also replaced it with one of its own vile offspring. Imagine the shock of the human parents when they wake up and go to cuddle their child. Meanwhile, the troll escapes to its cave where it will rear the young captive to work as its slave for life.

A hostile troll is a dangerous enemy. Powerful and cruel, it relishes bringing torment and grief to country folk, luring people to a horrible death or snatching sleeping babies from their cots. It is a supernatural trickster that dwells in permanent gloom and raids defenseless villages at night. Although it resembles a human, it is ugly, misshapen and coated with thick hair. A troll's greatest fear is sunlight, which causes it to turn to stone. If it can be fooled into forgetting the coming dawn, a troll's wicked career will be at an end.

WHERE IN THE WORLD?

Trolls are widespread in Scandinavia, particularly Norway, Sweden and Denmark and the remote Faroe Islands. The largest trolls, however, originally came from Iceland.

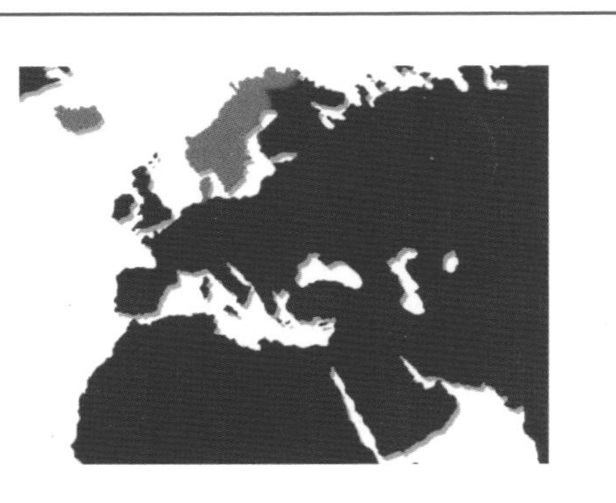

DID YOU KNOW?

- In J. R. R. Tolkien's books, *The Hobbit* and *The Lord of the Rings*, trolls are savage thugs often employed by the forces of evil as shock troops. Tough and long-lived, their greatest weaknesses are their own stupidity and fear of sunlight.
- In Icelandic myths, trolls have only one eye.
- Some myths talk of trolls having two or even three heads—the more heads, the higher the troll's status.

BASILISK

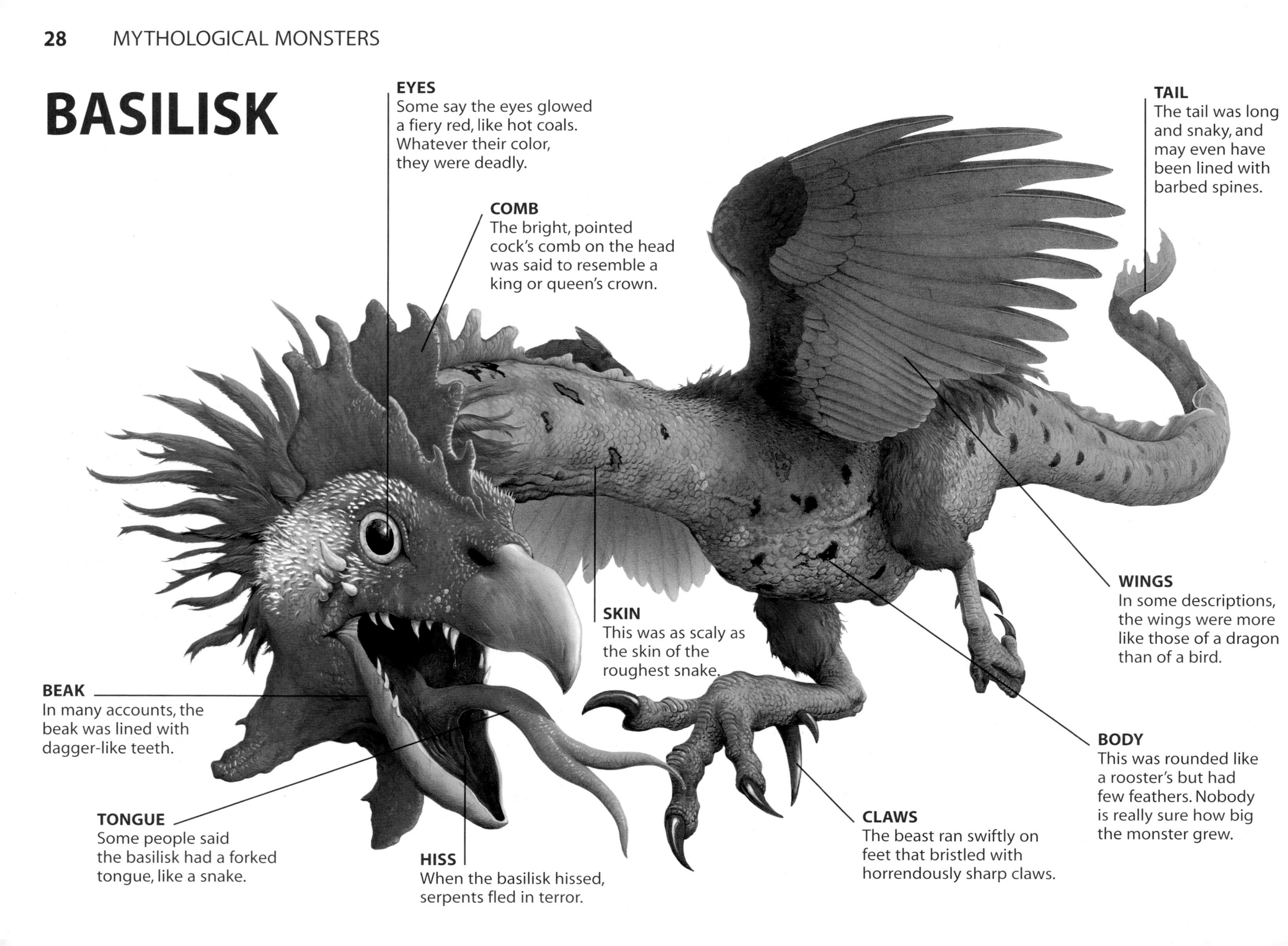
EYES
Some say the eyes glowed a fiery red, like hot coals. Whatever their color, they were deadly.
COMB
The bright, pointed cock's comb on the head was said to resemble a king or queen's crown.
TAIL
The tail was long and snaky, and may even have been lined with barbed spines.
SKIN
This was as scaly as the skin of the roughest snake.
WINGS
In some descriptions, the wings were more like those of a dragon than of a bird.
BEAK
In many accounts, the beak was lined with dagger-like teeth.
TONGUE
Some people said the basilisk had a forked tongue, like a snake.
HISS
When the basilisk hissed, serpents fled in terror.
CLAWS
The beast ran swiftly on feet that bristled with horrendously sharp claws.
BODY
This was rounded like a rooster's but had few feathers. Nobody is really sure how big the monster grew.

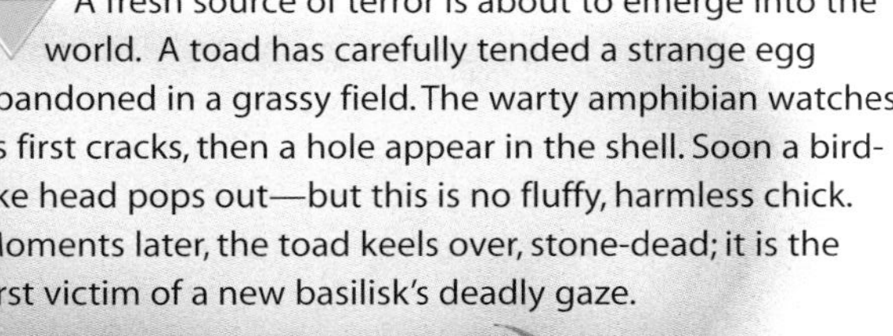

A fresh source of terror is about to emerge into the world. A toad has carefully tended a strange egg abandoned in a grassy field. The warty amphibian watches as first cracks, then a hole appear in the shell. Soon a bird-like head pops out—but this is no fluffy, harmless chick. Moments later, the toad keels over, stone-dead; it is the first victim of a new basilisk's deadly gaze.

The basilisk was a horrific mix of reptile and bird. It was said to be hatched from a freak egg laid by a cockerel, an egg that was then incubated by a toad. With their snake-like bodies, cockerel heads and stumpy wings, basilisks had terrifying magical powers. Just the stare of a basilisk could kill people, as could its foul poisonous breath. It polluted waterways and turned green, fertile farmland into nothing but barren desert. Rocks would shatter if the basilisk brushed against them. There were few ways to kill a basilisk. Weasels were said to be immune to basilisk magic and poison, and if a basilisk was confronted with a mirror, it would be killed by its own reflection.

WHERE IN THE WORLD?

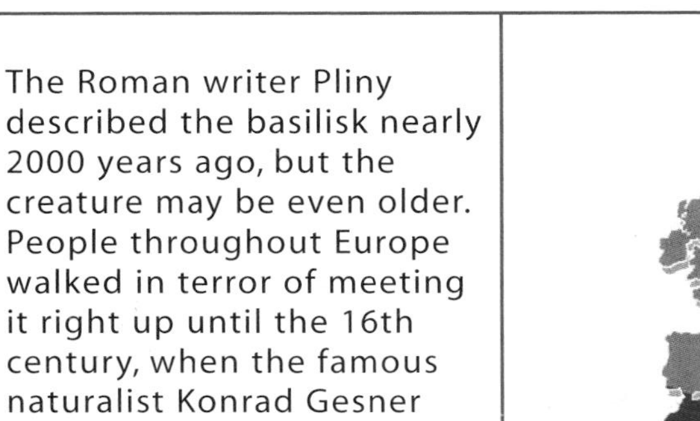

The Roman writer Pliny described the basilisk nearly 2000 years ago, but the creature may be even older. People throughout Europe walked in terror of meeting it right up until the 16th century, when the famous naturalist Konrad Gesner denounced it as "gossip."

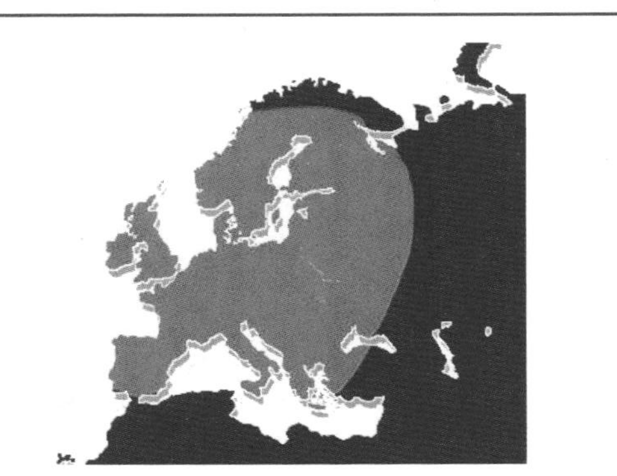

DID YOU KNOW?

- In Warsaw in Poland in 1587, a basilisk was blamed for killing two small girls in a cellar. Reportedly, a "volunteer" prisoner sent down into the cellar killed the creature with a mirror.
- The basilisk myth may come from early reports of hooded cobras, venomous Indian snakes that rear up and flare a hood of skin. The idea that a weasel can kill a basilisk may come from tales of the mongoose, a small mammal that preys on cobras.

CERBERUS

MANE
A mane of vipers' heads seethes around Cerberus' neck. In moments of aggression, this mass of snakes bristles and hisses in expectation of violence.

SERPENT TAIL
In the most terrifying portrayals of Cerberus, its tail consists of a serpent whose head rears up and springs into the attack. In other versions, Cerberus has either one or three dragon tails, each bearing a vicious spike.

JAWS
The jaws dribble venomous foam and a foul stench pours from the mouths. The dreadful teeth tear at pitiful victims condemned to punishment.

CLAWS
Some descriptions of Cerberus claim that the clawed feet are used to rip and flay the bodies of people who were greedy in life.

Cerberus is a particularly ancient mythical "hell hound"—his name is first seen in literature dating from around 700 BC. He is also the ultimate guard-dog. In Greek mythology, this three-headed beast presided over the entrance to the Underworld, preventing the unfortunate dead from ever escaping back into the the world of the living. Each terrifying head had powerful jaws that dripped poisonous saliva. A crop of snakes on the top of the heads added to Cerberus' ferocity.

The Underworld: In ancient myth, the dead were brought to the bank of the River Styx by the god Hermes. The only way to cross the Styx was to pay the hideous ferryman, Charon. Those who couldn't pay, or who were unburied, were doomed to wander the dismal shore of Styx for eternity. On the far bank, the souls passed Cerberus (left), who made sure they did not flee back to the land of the living. Once inside the gates of hell the souls were judged for their behavior in life: the good passed to the eternal paradise of the Elysian Fields; while the guilty were doomed to everlasting torment in Tartarus.

WHERE IN THE WORLD?

The Ancient Greeks believed that the Underworld lay at the center of the Earth and was accessible through certain entrances. The most famous of these were at Heraclea on the Black Sea and via the River Acheron in Thesprotia.

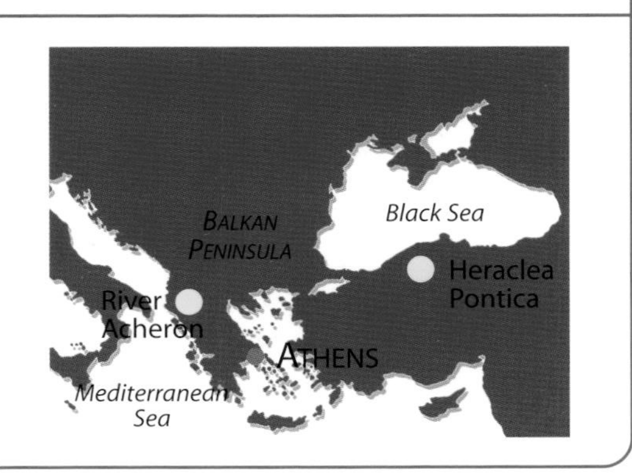

DID YOU KNOW?

- Cerberus' name probably stems from the Greek *ker berethrou*, meaning "demon of the pit".
- The Ancient Greeks were buried with a coin either in the mouth or placed in the grave because they believed their souls had to pay Charon to cross the River Styx.
- When Hercules captured Cerberus, drips of foam from its slavering jaws and venom from its mane of snakes' heads fell on the ground. From these drips sprouted the poisonous plant aconite, commonly known as wolfsbane.
- Theseus, famous for killing the Minotaur, spent four years trapped in hell, continually savaged by Cerberus. He was freed when Hercules captured Cerberus.
- Cerberus's mother was the half-woman, half-serpent, Echidne.

CHIMAERA

GOAT'S HEAD
From the middle of the beast's back grew another head, that of a goat.

TAIL
In place of a tail was the slender body and head of a fork-tongued serpent. As in a real snake, its fangs were laden with venom.

CLAWS
Each foot was equipped with a set of vicious claws, capable of raking the flesh of victims.

HEAD
From the front the Chimaera was all jaws and teeth, for its chief head was that of a ferocious lion.

Born with a trio of beastly heads, the Chimaera was a hateful and bloodthirsty monster from the pages of old Greek mythology. Three beasts rolled into one, the creature was part lion, part goat, and part snake. Each head could act independently and face different directions. Worst of all, the lion breathed out horrifying spouts of flame. It terrorized the people of an ancient territory called Lycia until a hero came to save them. The Chimaera was born to two hideous parents, Typhon and Echidna. Typhon was a winged monster with 100 heads and Echidna was half woman, half snake. The slayer of their awful "child" was the warrior Bellerophon, who rode into battle against the Chimaera on the famous winged horse, Pegasus.

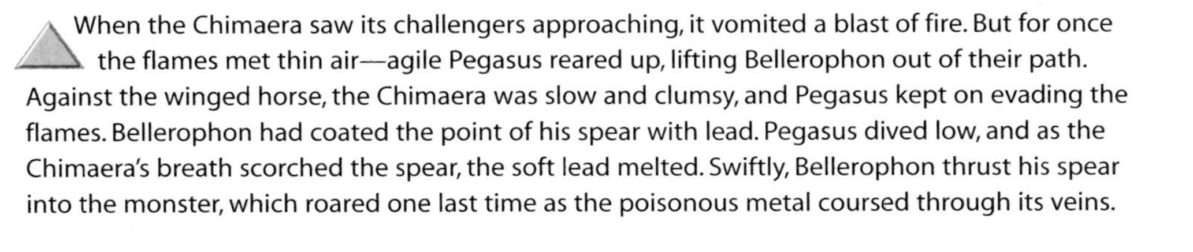

When the Chimaera saw its challengers approaching, it vomited a blast of fire. But for once the flames met thin air—agile Pegasus reared up, lifting Bellerophon out of their path. Against the winged horse, the Chimaera was slow and clumsy, and Pegasus kept on evading the flames. Bellerophon had coated the point of his spear with lead. Pegasus dived low, and as the Chimaera's breath scorched the spear, the soft lead melted. Swiftly, Bellerophon thrust his spear into the monster, which roared one last time as the poisonous metal coursed through its veins.

WHERE IN THE WORLD?

The Chimaera was said to dwell in Lycia, in the south of modern Turkey. About 2500 years ago, Lycia was the scene of fierce struggles between Persia and Greece. Its culture was greatly influenced by both civilizations.

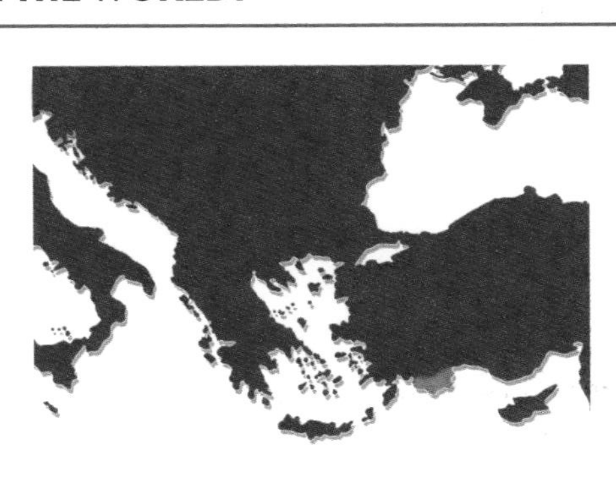

DID YOU KNOW?

- The Chimaera represented the power and danger of storm clouds. Its roar was like thunder, and the fire it spat out was like lightning.
- A sea fish with a large head, big eyes and a whip-like tail is also called a chimaera. It's a mixture, like its mythical namesake. It has some features in common with sharks and other cartilaginous (sinewy) fish, but other features in common with the main class of fish, the bony fishes.

CYCLOPS

HAIR
Sprouting wildly from the cyclops' head, the dirty, matted hair is infested with lice.
EYE
One huge, watchful eye stares from the center of the cyclops' forehead.
TEETH
When the cyclops wants a snack, he rips up humans with his big, pointed teeth.
ARMS
Bulging with muscles, the long arms pound out metal and shift stone blocks with ease.
CLAWS
Instead of nails, hooked claws grow from the fingers and toes. If the cyclops is in a bad mood, these make formidable weapons.
FEET
The whole ground shakes when the cyclops stamps around on his massive feet.

Odysseus waited patiently for the Cyclops to fall asleep. Then the hero sharpened a stake and heated it in the fire. Driving the weapon into the scary giant's eye, Odysseus twisted the stake around, blinding Polyphemus. The survivors escaped the next day, clinging to the bellies of the cyclops' sheep as he sent them out to graze.

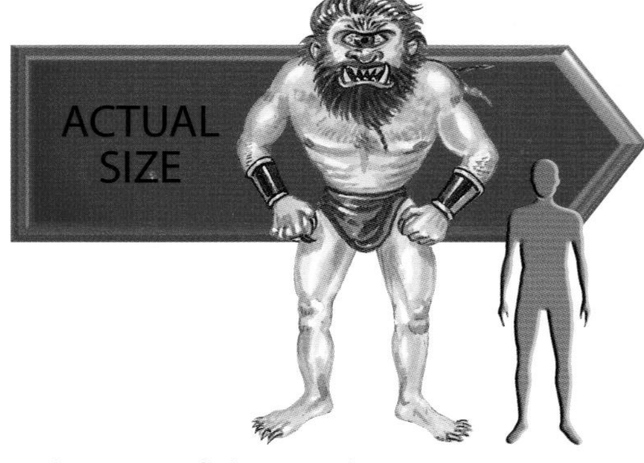

The single eye of the cyclops stares menacingly from its horrible, hairy face. This cruel, watchful giant can smash a human to pieces with a single flick of the wrist. In Greek mythology, the first cyclopes were three brothers called Steropes, Brontes and Arges, sons of Ge (Mother Earth) and the god Uranus. They were blacksmiths by trade. The last race of cyclopes were brutish shepherds who lived squalid lives in dingy caves in Sicily, tending their flocks and tearing intruders apart. They communicated with grunts and roars. The cyclops Polyphemus was the most dreadful of all. When Odysseus and his men turned up at his cave, Polyphemus imprisoned them. Dashing out the brains of two men a day, he ate the men whole.

WHERE IN THE WORLD?

Cyclopes lived in the regions of Thrace in northeast Greece, in Lycia in southwest Turkey, and on the island of Crete. They worked in Hephaestus' forge on Lemnos, and built the cities of Mycenae and Tiryns. Later tales place them on Mount Etna in Sicily.

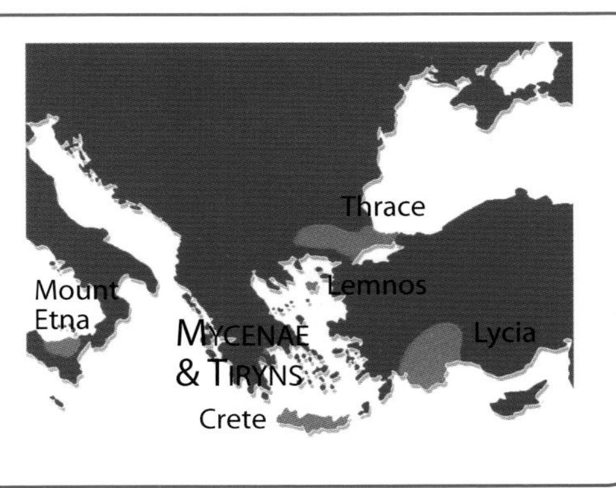

DID YOU KNOW?

- The word "cyclops"comes from the Greek words kyklos ("circle") and ops ("eye"). The names of the cyclopes Brontes, Steropes and Arges meant "thunder," "lightning bolt," and "lightning flash."
- The cyclops myth may have its origins in an ancient guild of Greek metal-workers in Thrace, who had circles tattooed on their foreheads.
- Some people believe that the legend of the cyclopes arose when the Ancient Greeks first encountered elephants.

FENRIR

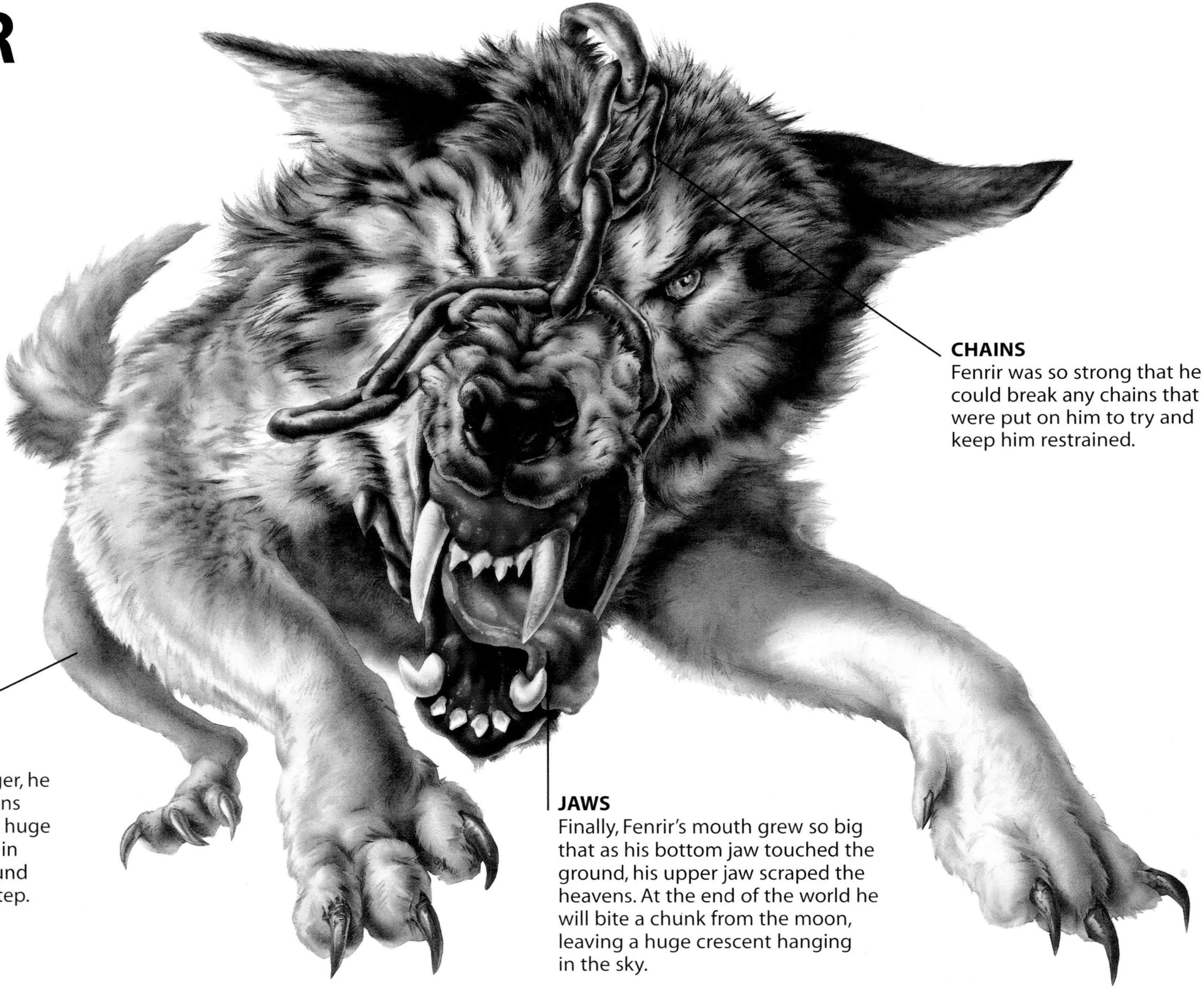

CHAINS
Fenrir was so strong that he could break any chains that were put on him to try and keep him restrained.

LEGS
As Fenrir grew ever larger, he could straddle mountains and span lakes with his huge legs, and as he roamed in search of food, the ground trembled at each pawstep.

JAWS
Finally, Fenrir's mouth grew so big that as his bottom jaw touched the ground, his upper jaw scraped the heavens. At the end of the world he will bite a chunk from the moon, leaving a huge crescent hanging in the sky.

The broken links of Laeding still rattling around his shoulders, Fenrir storms into a small village in Midgard. He's now so huge that the thatched cottages look like toy houses, and their beams shatter like matchsticks beneath his massive paws. Screaming in horror at the spectacle, the human inhabitants flee for their lives. But as Fenrir rips through the thatched roofs with his great teeth, some move too slowly to escape their fate and are gobbled up in a flash.

Feared for his savage nature and ferocious appetite, this terrifying, devouring wolf of Norse mythology grew so strong that ordinary chains couldn't hold him. He was one of three children spawned by the trickster god Loki and a forbidding giantess. Fenrir grew so rapidly that even the powerful Norse gods, or Æsir, began to fear for their lives. Finally, the *Æsir* forged two heavy iron chains, and twice they challenged Fenrir to a test of strength and bound him. But as soon as the chains were in place, Fenrir simply shrugged his great shoulders and broke his bonds with ease. He was finally bound by a magical ribbon called Glepnir. Norse myth predicts Fenrir is destined to escape at Ragnorak—the end of the world—when he will swallow the sun and then kill Odin, king of the Norse gods.

WHERE IN THE WORLD?

Fenrir has his origins in the mythology of the Norse people or Vikings, who lived in Sweden, Norway and Denmark up to 2000 years ago. Later in their reign, they also populated Iceland, and the area under their influence is sometimes referred to as Scandinavia.

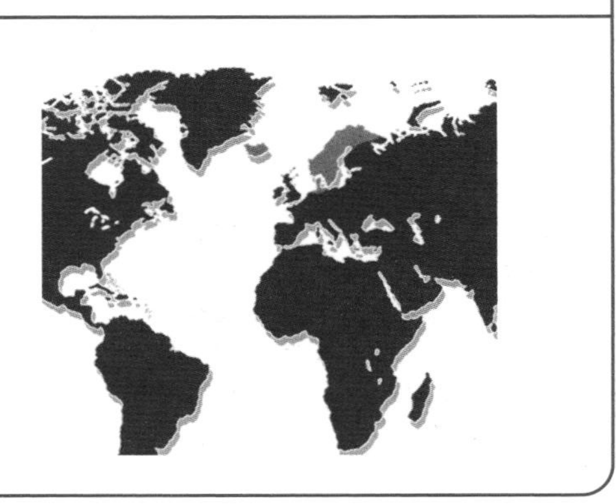

DID YOU KNOW?

- Glepnir, the magical ribbon that imprisons Fenrir, was made from the sound of a cat's footsteps, the roots of a mountain, the sinews of a bear, the beard of a woman, the breath of a fish and the spit of a bird.

- Norse myth predicts at Ragnorak, Fenrir's bonds will fall off and he will join forces with the other monsters against the Æsir. The great wolf will fight Odin and swallow him whole, only to have his jaws ripped apart by Odin's son Vidir.

GORGON

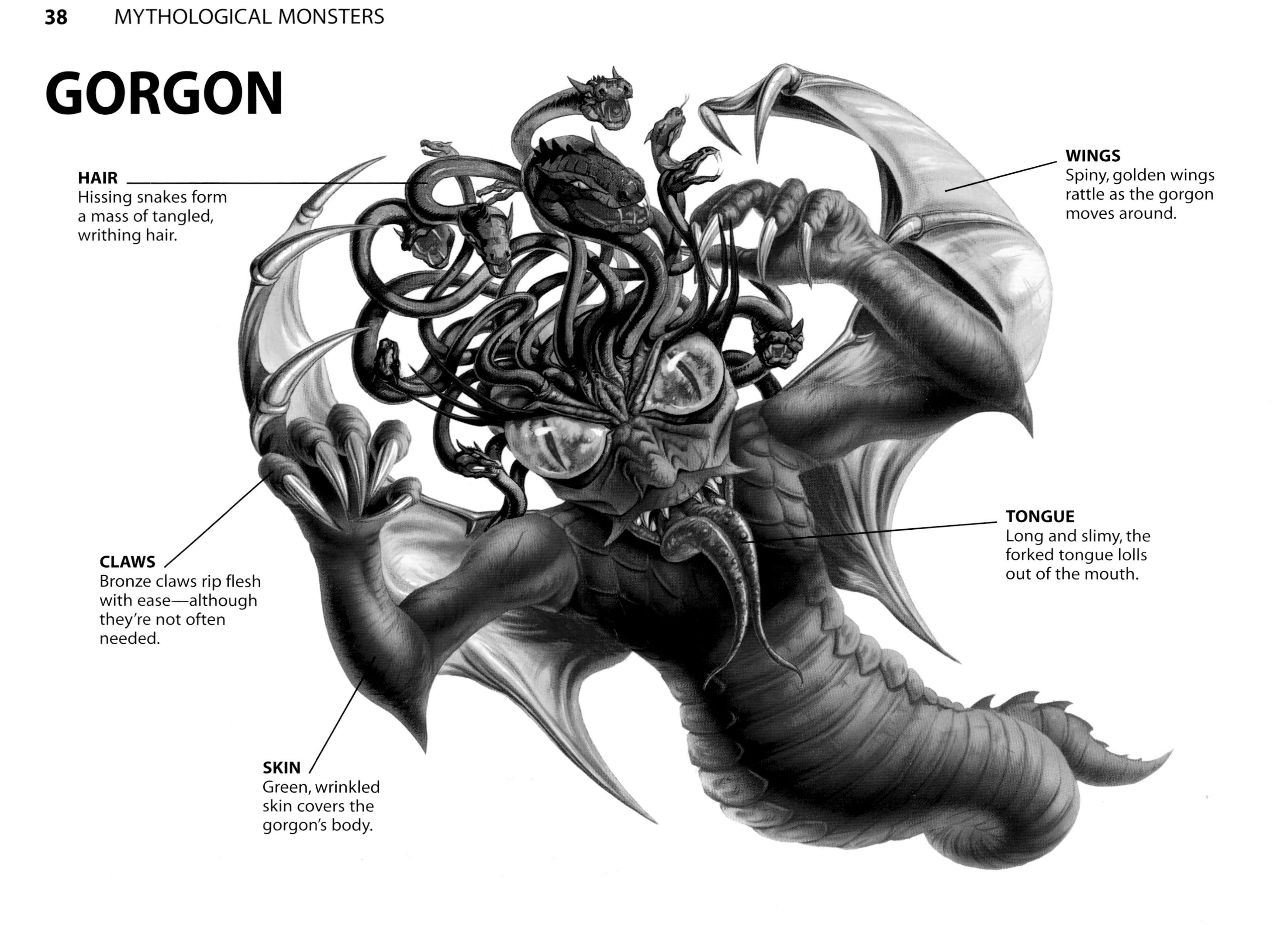
HAIR
Hissing snakes form a mass of tangled, writhing hair.
WINGS
Spiny, golden wings rattle as the gorgon moves around.
CLAWS
Bronze claws rip flesh with ease—although they're not often needed.
TONGUE
Long and slimy, the forked tongue lolls out of the mouth.
SKIN
Green, wrinkled skin covers the gorgon's body.

A gorgon is such a hideous spectacle, that one glance is enough to turn onlookers to stone. The gorgons were not always vile monsters. Once they were beautiful sisters, until Medusa offended the goddess Athena by seducing the sea god, Poseidon, in one of her temples. Athena was furious, and turned the sisters into hideous creatures. The hero Perseus killed the gorgon Medusa with help from the gods and from a highly polished shield. The shield acted like a mirror, which meant he did not have to look directly into Medusa's face. Perseus then used Medusa's severed head to turn his own enemies into statues.

Medusa is the only mortal gorgon. Her name means"the cunning one". In some versions of the myth, she is the only one of the three who can turn people to stone, but other versions say that all the gorgon sisters have this power.

Stheno and Euryale are Medusa's sisters, destined to share her awful fate. Both these gorgons are immortal, and in some versions of the myth, are slightly less hideous than their sister. The name Stheno means "the mighty one", and Euryale "the wide-roaming one".

Crumbling stone statues litter the gorgons' dreary lair, the petrified remains of onlookers who fell victim to the sisters' terrible powers. Humans aren't the only ones susceptible—even animals are turned to stone by the gruesome spectacle.

WHERE IN THE WORLD?

The ancient Greeks believed the gorgons lived in the mythical land of the Hyperboreans, beyond the north wind on the shores of the ocean that encircled the Earth. The sources place this land as being the coast of Russia, Scandinavia or northeastern Europe.

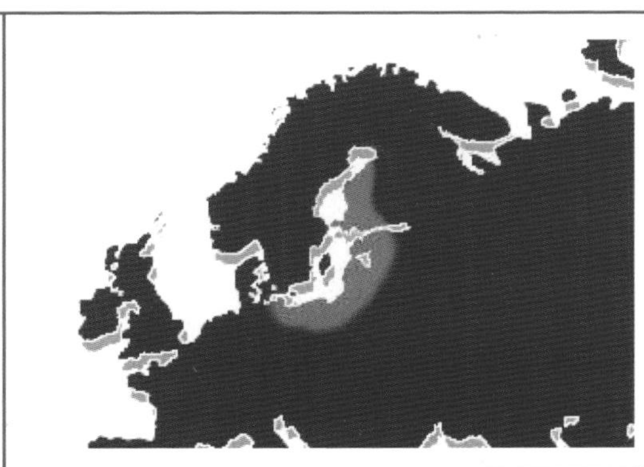

DID YOU KNOW?

- According to legend when Perseus cut off Medusa's head, the winged horse Pegasus and a fully armed warrior called Chrysaor sprang from her body.
- As Perseus flew back to Greece, drops of Medusa's blood fell into the sea, instantly turning into coral known as gorgonia. More drops fell on the desert, where they became snakes.
- Athene gave two vials of gorgon blood to Asclepius, the founder of Greek medicine. She filled one from the veins on the left of Medusa's body, and the other from the veins on the right. Blood from the left side could raise the dead, while that from the right destroyed life.

GRIFFIN

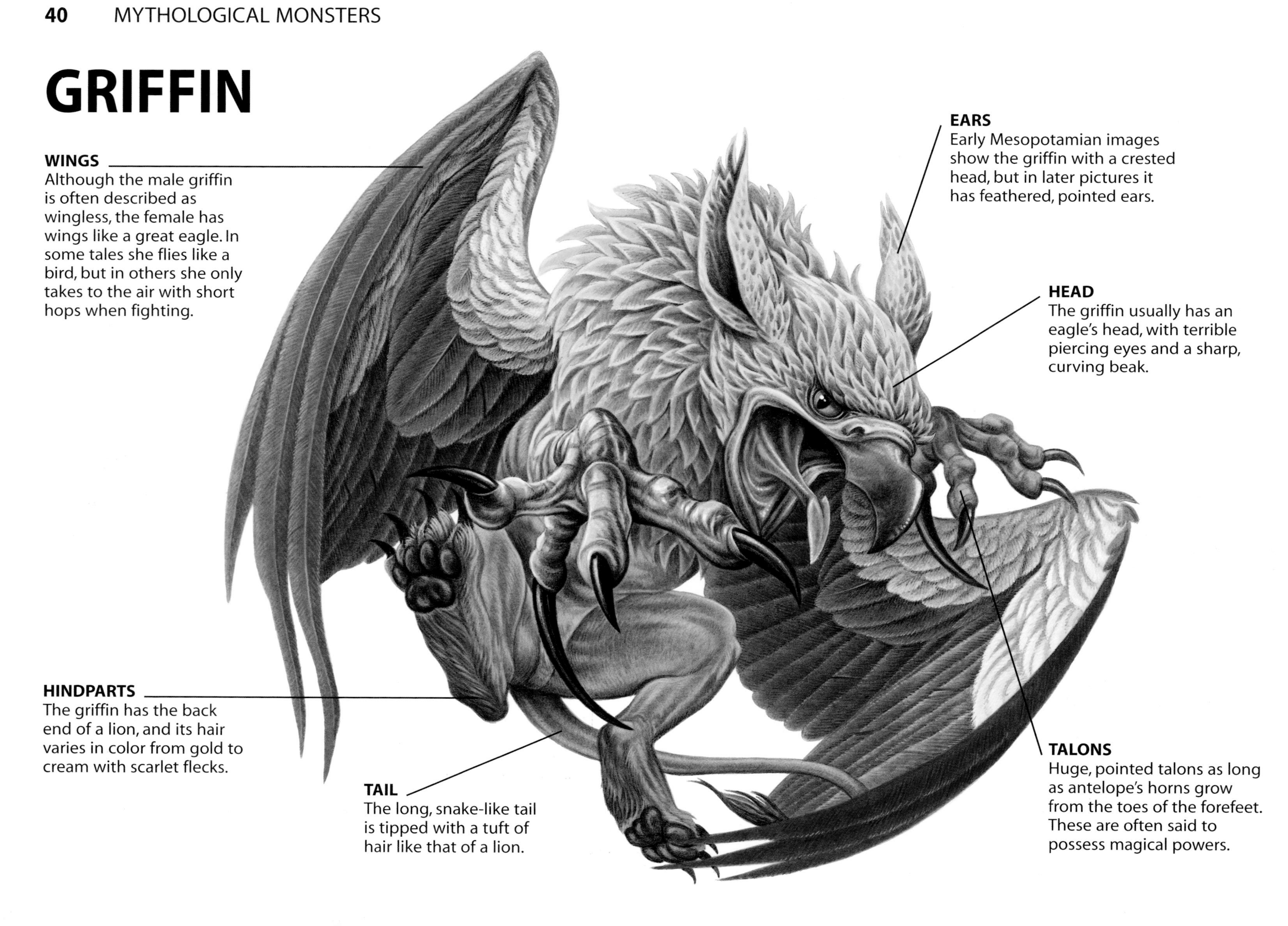

WINGS
Although the male griffin is often described as wingless, the female has wings like a great eagle. In some tales she flies like a bird, but in others she only takes to the air with short hops when fighting.

HINDPARTS
The griffin has the back end of a lion, and its hair varies in color from gold to cream with scarlet flecks.

TAIL
The long, snake-like tail is tipped with a tuft of hair like that of a lion.

EARS
Early Mesopotamian images show the griffin with a crested head, but in later pictures it has feathered, pointed ears.

HEAD
The griffin usually has an eagle's head, with terrible piercing eyes and a sharp, curving beak.

TALONS
Huge, pointed talons as long as antelope's horns grow from the toes of the forefeet. These are often said to possess magical powers.

This ferocious mythological beast has the head, wings and forelegs of an eagle, and the hindquarters of a lion. Given to attacking other animals at will, it's also said to tear up humans on sight with its slashing claws and tearing beak. The griffin is a colossally powerful predator that can carry off a yoke of oxen in its claws—in some medieval accounts, it is stronger than eight lions and 100 eagles. It also hoards gold and emeralds, fiercely attacking anyone who tries to steal from its nest.

Many griffins were said to live in the ancient land of Scythia, north of the Black Sea—an area rich in gold and jewels. Digging up these treasures with their claws, they used them to line their nests. The Arimaspians wanted these riches, too and often rode on horseback into battle with the griffins. As a result, griffins attacked horses whenever they could. Gripping with their scythe-like claws, they hacked in with the hooked bill, leaving terrible, bloody wounds.

WHERE IN THE WORLD?

Griffins were thought to live in various parts of the Near and Middle East, from Egypt, Greece and Turkey through to Syria, Iraq, Iran and Armenia. They were also strongly associated with India and southern parts of the former Soviet Union.

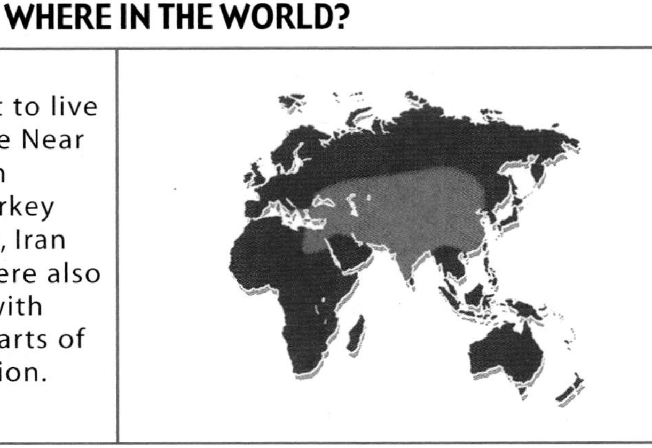

DID YOU KNOW?

- Artifacts from Ancient Greece sometimes show the griffin with a mane of tightly coiled curls.
- One Norse legend tells of Prince Hagen, who was carried away to a griffin's nest. Fortunately he found a suit of armor and managed to kill the young griffins as they attacked.
- The female griffin lays eggs like those of an eagle. Her young are far more gentle than an adret.

HARPY

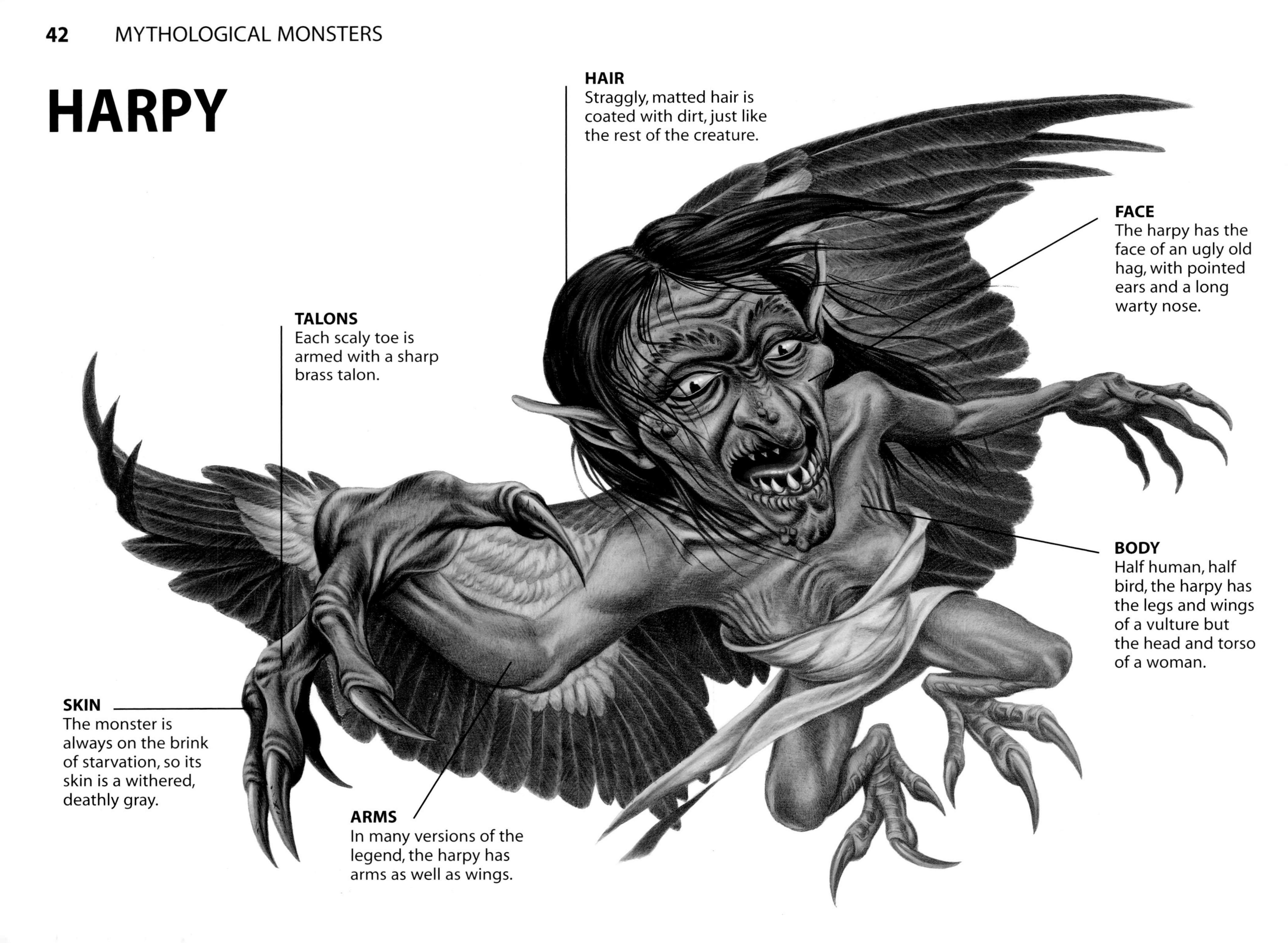
HAIR
Straggly, matted hair is coated with dirt, just like the rest of the creature.
FACE
The harpy has the face of an ugly old hag, with pointed ears and a long warty nose.
TALONS
Each scaly toe is armed with a sharp brass talon.
BODY
Half human, half bird, the harpy has the legs and wings of a vulture but the head and torso of a woman.
SKIN
The monster is always on the brink of starvation, so its skin is a withered, deathly gray.
ARMS
In many versions of the legend, the harpy has arms as well as wings.

Reeking of dirt and decay, these ghastly females have the body and head of a screeching hag and the wings and tail of a scavenging vulture. They leave a horrible stench wherever they go. The Harpies first appeared in Greek legend, and they were linked with the terrifying power of storms and gales. They were also believed to carry off the souls of the dead, transporting them to the Underworld.

In exchange for his eyesight, King Phineus had accepted from Zeus the power to see into the future. But later, the king offended Zeus by giving away the gods' secret plans. In punishment, Zeus sent the harpies to plague him for all time. Their thieving habits doomed the king to an eternity of awful hunger. A visit from the Argonauts finally saved blind Phineus. The roving Greek heroes promised to help him in return for his advice. Phineus threw a lavish banquet, and soon the harpies swooped screeching from the skies, circling the table and grabbing handfuls of food. Two of the Argonauts, Zetes and Calais, had powerful wings. They drew their weapons and flew after the harpies, chasing them away.

WHERE IN THE WORLD?

Classical legends say that the harpies were expelled from Thrace by the Argonauts. They were forced to take permanent refuge on a group of islands in the Ionian Sea, west of Greece, which later became known as the Strophades.

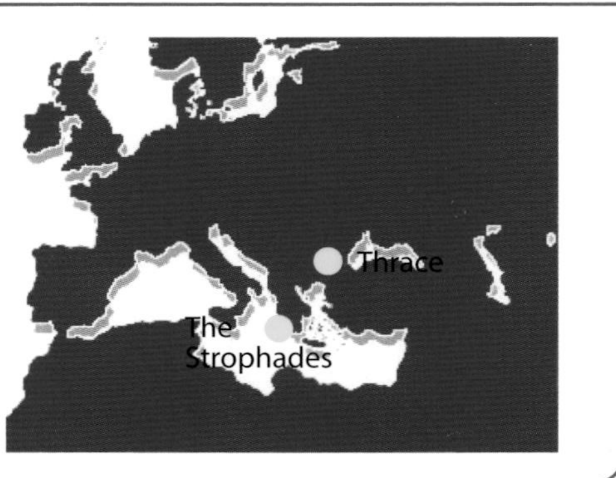

DID YOU KNOW?

- Although the harpy is constantly hungry and is always on the verge of starvation, it is an immortal being, incapable of ever dying.
- Legend says when the harpies fled from Thrace, one fell exhausted into a river in the Peloponnese in Greece. The river is now named Harpyes.
- In some versions of the harpy myth, these monsters have the claws of a lion and the ears of a bear.
- The harpy has a namesake that lives in the tropical forests of South America: the harpy eagle. This rare, giant bird of prey has a menacing beak and deeply curved talons. It is powerful enough to snatch sloths and monkeys from the treetops.
- Four harpies appear in some stories: Aello, Celaeno, Ocypete and Podarge. Translated, their names mean "rain-squall," "storm-dark," "swift-flying," and "swift-foot."

HYDRA

BODY
In some tales the Hydra looked like a huge water serpent, but in others it had the body of a dog.

IMMORTAL HEAD
The central head was larger than the others and could never be completely destroyed. In some versions of the tale, it was made of gold.

MORTAL HEAD
The Hydra was usually shown with eight mortal heads, but whenever one was severed, two sprung up in its place. In some descriptions, it had as many as 100 heads.

FANGS
Long, hollow fangs dripping with toxic venom protruded from every mouth.

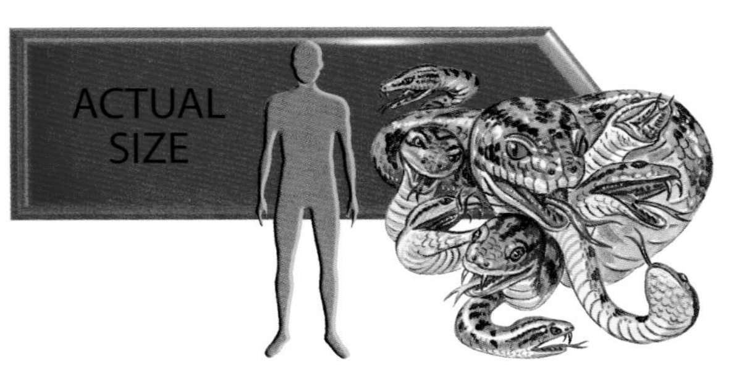

This fearsome, many-headed water serpent lurked in the marshes of Lerna in Ancient Greece. The Hydra stopped local farmers from reaching the fresh water they needed for their plains, and also emerged to attack the villagers and their cattle. Its poisonous breath and toxic venom killed anyone who came near. The Hydra's central head was immortal, and if one of the outer, mortal, heads was cut off, two more immediately grew in its place. Seemingly invincible, it was finally slain by Hercules.

Wearing his protective lionskin and holding his breath against the lethal fumes, Hercules attacked. But as fast as he severed each mortal head, two new ones grew in its place. He was simply making the monster more powerful. So he told Iolaus to sear each bleeding neck-stump with a blazing torch—until finally only the huge immortal head remained. Crushing this with his club, he tore it, still hissing, from the Hydra's body and buried it deep in the ground.

WHERE IN THE WORLD?

After making its home under a plane tree at the source of the River Amymone in southern Greece, the Hydra roamed the treacherous swamps of Lerna.

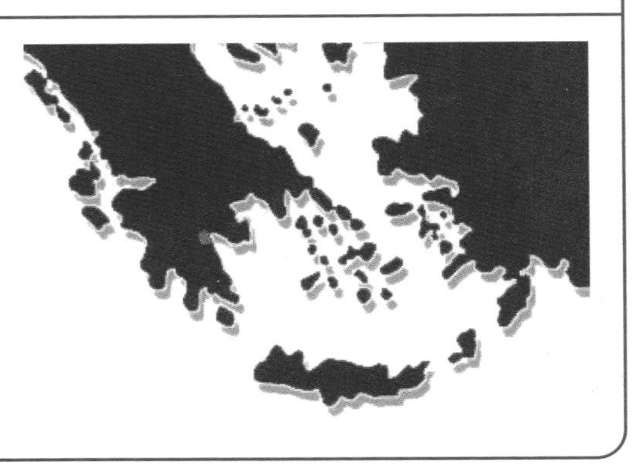

DID YOU KNOW?

- The term hydra is sometimes used to describe a complex problem where each possible solution only leads to more difficulties. It is also used to describe anything that is difficult to root out and destroy.
- The Greek astronomer Ptolemy named a constellation of stars Hydra, because it looked like a water snake.
- Serpents feature in myths more often than any other creature.

KRAKEN

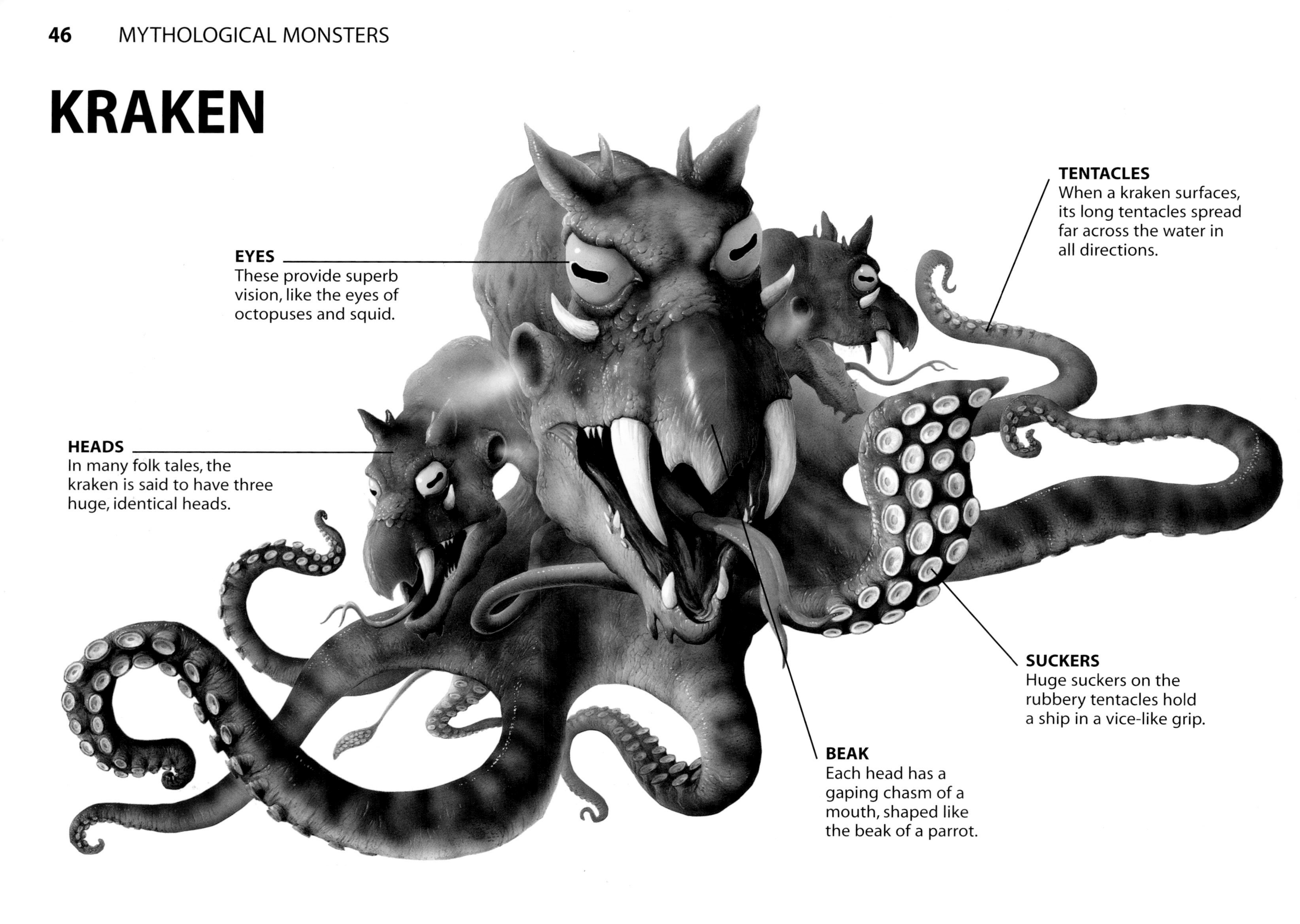
EYES
These provide superb vision, like the eyes of octopuses and squid.
HEADS
In many folk tales, the kraken is said to have three huge, identical heads.
TENTACLES
When a kraken surfaces, its long tentacles spread far across the water in all directions.
SUCKERS
Huge suckers on the rubbery tentacles hold a ship in a vice-like grip.
BEAK
Each head has a gaping chasm of a mouth, shaped like the beak of a parrot.

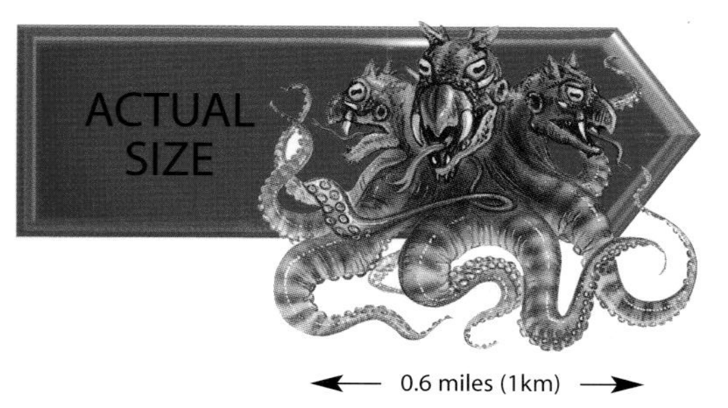

Since medieval times, sailors and fishermen from western Europe—especially Scandinavia—have told of a vast, tentacled sea monster that lives in the ocean depths. The kraken is a mountain of a creature, dwarfing the largest of whales. In one book on the natural history of Norway, published in 1754, the Bishop of Bergen even claimed that the monster's body was almost 1.5 miles (2.5km) in circumference.

In the seas off northern Europe, a travel-weary captain sights land at last. His charts make no reference to the strangely rounded islands, but he trusts his eyes and steers his ship toward them. But as he draws closer, the captain realizes his mistake with horror. The "islands" erupt from the sea to reveal a huge kraken. The waking monster seizes the ship in a mighty tentacle and plunges it beneath the boiling waves. Grasping one of the crew with another, it lifts him, screaming, into a gaping beak.

WHERE IN THE WORLD?

Most of the legends tell us the kraken lived around the coasts of Scandinavia, especially in the deep waters off Norway. But similar tales also come from other coastal areas of Europe.

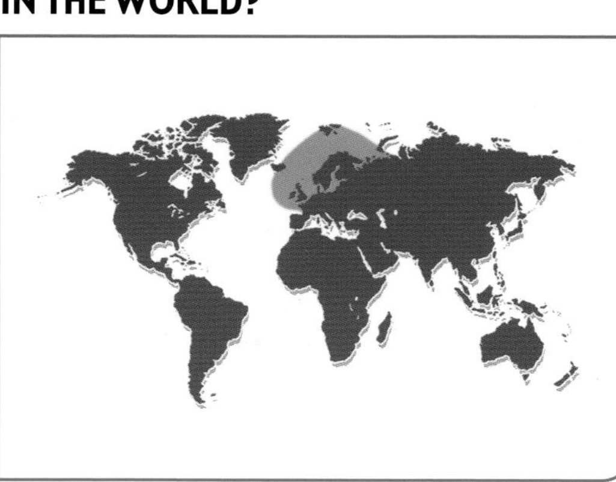

DID YOU KNOW?

- In some tales, the kraken has 1000 tentacles and 10 mouths.
- There are reports of accidental kraken strandings. In 1680, a young kraken supposedly died after it was caught on the reefs off Alstadhang in Norway. And in 1775, another was found on the Isle of Bute in Scotland.
- The English 19th-century poet Alfred, Lord Tennyson wrote a poem, "The Kraken," inspired by the myths.

MANTICORE

STEALTH
The manticore often prowls menacingly through the forest and sneaks up on a victim with all the stealth of a big cat stalking its prey. But close to, it attacks head-on.

BODY
The beast has the body of a lion—and the strength to match.

CLAWS
Dried blood cakes the dagger-like claws, which can slash a person open with a single swipe.

TAIL
The monster has the long, segmented, arching tail of a gigantic scorpion—but the tip bristles with a cluster of venomous spines, not just one sting. At close quarters, the manticore wields its spiky club like a medieval knight's mace.

SPINES
When the manticore shoots spines from the club on the tip of its tail, new ones immediately grow in their place.

FACE
Filthy, tangled hair flows from the hideous human face like a cross between an unkempt beard and the mane of a mangy old lion.

TEETH
Three rows of long yellow teeth fill each jaw and interlock when the monster sinks them deep into a victim's body.

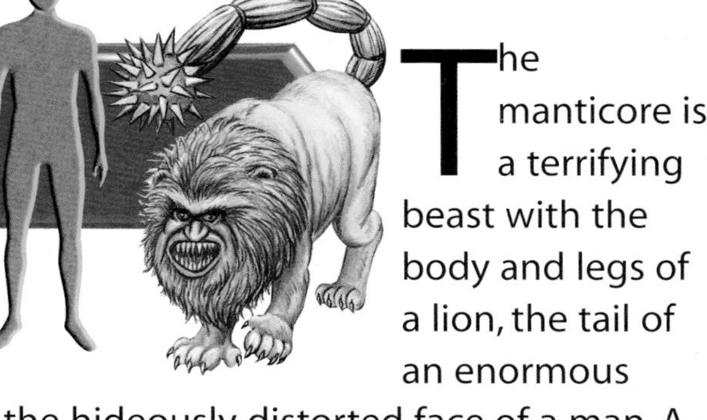

The manticore is a terrifying beast with the body and legs of a lion, the tail of an enormous scorpion and the hideously distorted face of a man. A merciless and ruthlessly efficient man-eater from which no victim ever escapes, it kills with wickedly sharp, flesh-ripping claws and teeth—and by firing spear-like spikes from the end of its tail. It originated in ancient Indian mythology, before entering medieval European folklore as the embodiment of evil. The first European account of the manticore is by a Greek doctor and traveller, Ctesias, who lived in the 4th century BC. He claims he saw the beast at the Persian court, and his horrifying description of it survives in later Greek and Roman writings.

A lone European merchant is on his way east to buy spices. Little does he know, but he'll never make it. The manticore springs straight for him, roaring and baring its ghastly teeth. Rooted to the spot with terror, the man barely has time to let out a strangled cry before the advancing beast is arching its tail over its head and firing a flurry of spines deep into his belly and chest. Searing pain instantly sweeps through his body.

Even as the traveler falls to the ground dying, the manticore starts to devour him and greedily gulps down great mouthfuls of the innocent merchant's body. The monster eats everything: the head and clothing—even the man's meager possessions.

WHERE IN THE WORLD?

Stories about the manticore originated in northern India, in the Himalayan foothills. Tigers once abounded in these remote regions. Travelers on long, lonely footpaths between isolated villages trod in constant dread of man-eaters.

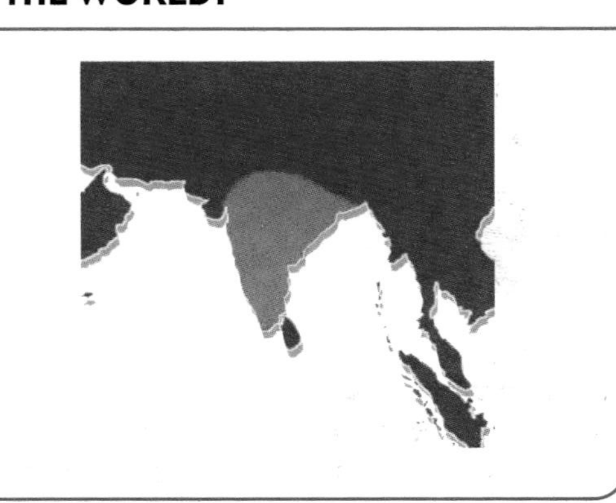

DID YOU KNOW?

- The word "manticore" comes from the ancient Persian word mardkhora, meaning "man-slayer".
- According to Spanish folklore, the mantiquera, or manticore, is a bearded werewolf that eats children. As recently as the 1930s, a group of peasants in a remote part of Spain attacked a traveler with a beard, believing that he was a mantiquera who had come to steal their babies by night, cut them up and eat them.

MINOTAUR

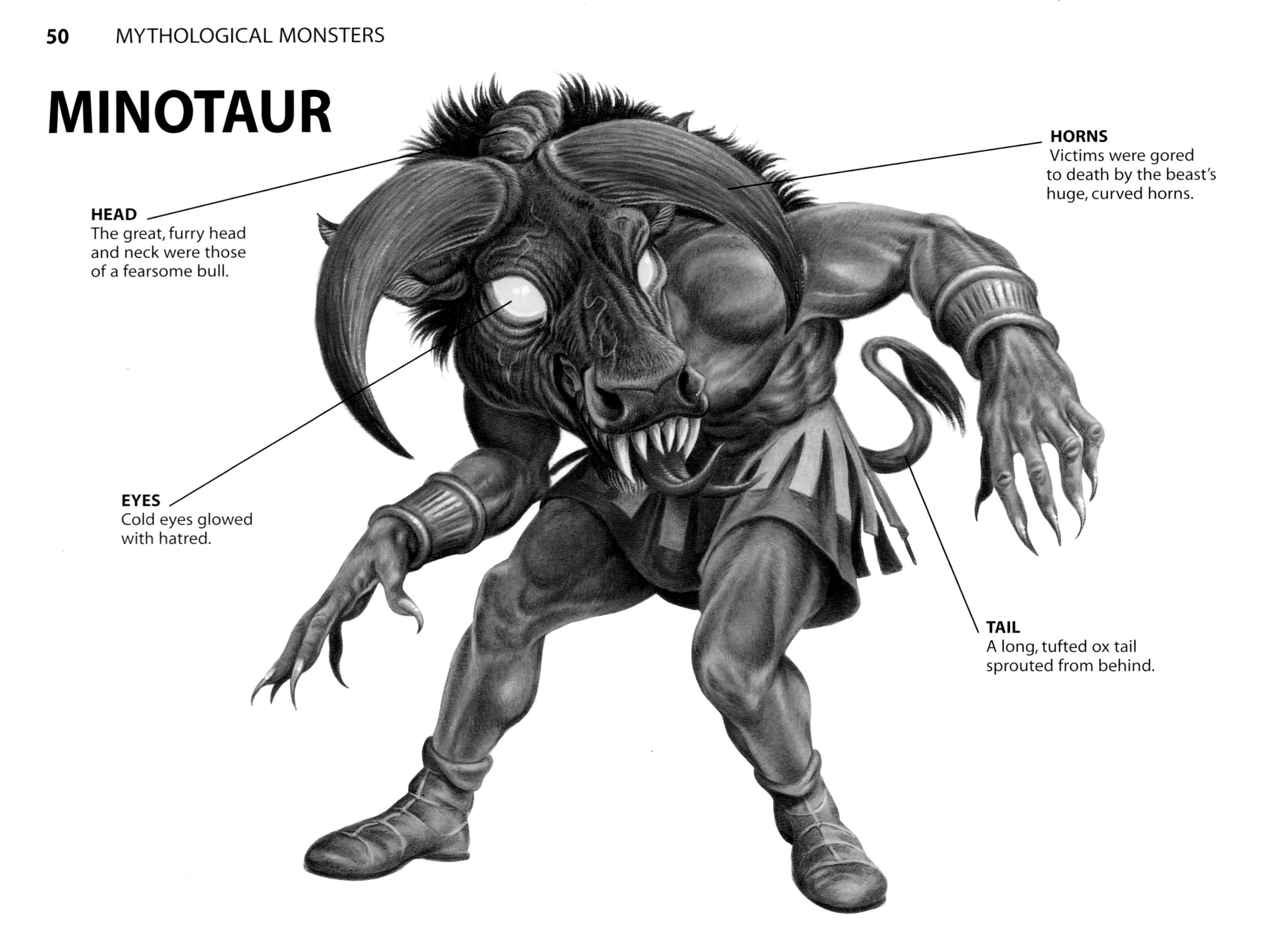
HEAD
The great, furry head and neck were those of a fearsome bull.
EYES
Cold eyes glowed with hatred.
HORNS
Victims were gored to death by the beast's huge, curved horns.
TAIL
A long, tufted ox tail sprouted from behind.

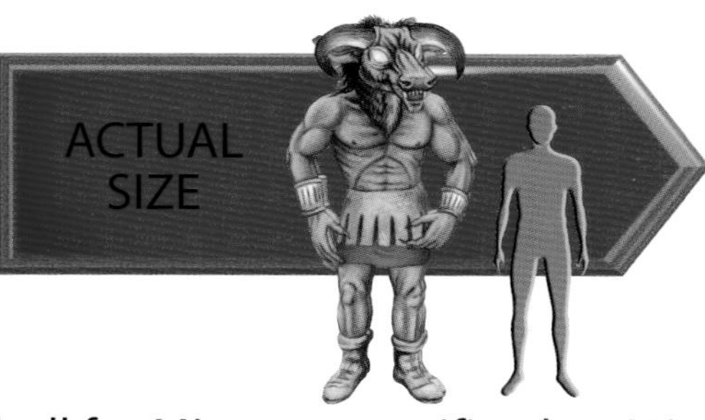

The Minotaur was born after King Minos angered the sea-god Poseidon. Poseidon had sent a snow-white bull for Minos to sacrifice, but Minos couldn't bring himself to kill the bull. Poseidon was furious, and punished Minos by making his wife, Queen Pasiphae, fall in love with the animal. Pasiphae produced a child with a grotesque bull's head and a taste for human flesh. Minos ordered the master craftsman Daedalus to make a vast underground maze to house the monster. The Minotaur was put inside, where it remained lost in the darkness. Every so often, human victims were forced into the maze as sacrifices. The Minotaur was finally vanquished by Theseus, one of the great Greek heroes.

1. Theseus and his companions were sent from Athens as a sacrifice. Forced into the Labyrinth, they faced a maze of dark passages. Quickly, Theseus revealed his plan to the terrified Athenians, and told them to stay near the entrance while he went in search of the Minotaur, armed with a sword and a ball of thread.

2. Tying the end of the thread firmly to a doorpost, Theseus cautiously picked his way through the tunnels of the maze, unraveling the ball as he went. He knew that, after killing the beast, he would be able to retrace his steps and escape the maze by following the thread.

3. Suddenly, the terrible beast was upon him, snorting and charging with horns lowered. A desperate fight ensued, until, summoning all his strength and courage, Theseus plunged the sword through the Minotaur's neck, severing its head from its body.

WHERE IN THE WORLD?

The mythical Minotaur was said to have lived at Knossos, on the island of Crete in the eastern Mediterranean. Theseus, who slew the beast, came from the city of Athens on the Greek mainland.

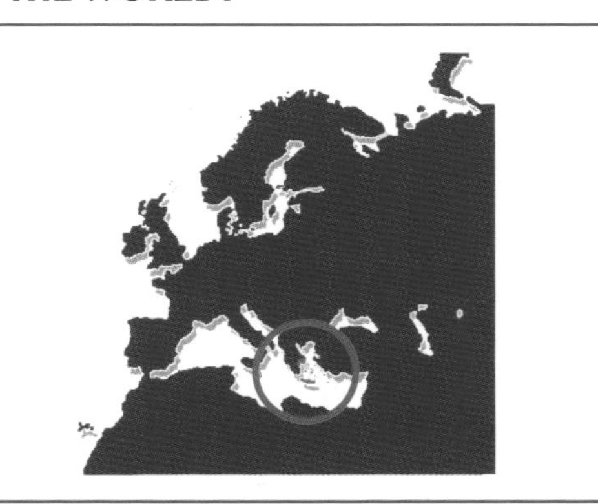

DID YOU KNOW?

- The story of Theseus slaying the Minotaur could be a symbolic version of real historical events, representing the Greek overthrow of Minoan power in 1450 BC.
- Artifacts from ancient Crete show athletes performing the death-defying bull-leaping ceremony. Each athlete would face a wild, charging bull, grasp its spiked horns, and vault or somersault over the animal's back.
- The Nemean lion was another Greek monster: a giant beast invulnerable to wounds.

ONI

HANDS
Onis are immensely strong, and can tear down walls with their sharp claws.

HORNS
Onis usually have three horns: either like those of a bull or taking the form of writhing snakes with venom-primed fangs.

FACE
Some gaki onis have the heads of cattle or horses, but most have human features—with three eyes and a hideous hole of a mouth that stretches from ear to ear.

FANGS
Onis have long, curved fangs like those of a tiger, and in some tales they are said to gorge on human flesh.

PANTS
In Chinese myth, a "Kimon" gate separates demons from the Earth—and as this faces the tiger of the zodiac, the oni usually wears tigerskin pants.

Whistling gaily as it works, this ghastly creature delights in tormenting the people of Japan, avoiding detection by flitting invisibly through the air or taking human form. Once a Shinto god, it became an evil spirit after Buddhism spread into Japan from China in the 6th century CE. In earthly guise it causes disasters, famine and disease, while its demonic form steals sinners' souls. Many Onis have green or red skin. They suffer continual hunger and often have enormous bellies. Hunting down sinners, they take them in a fiery chariot to hell.

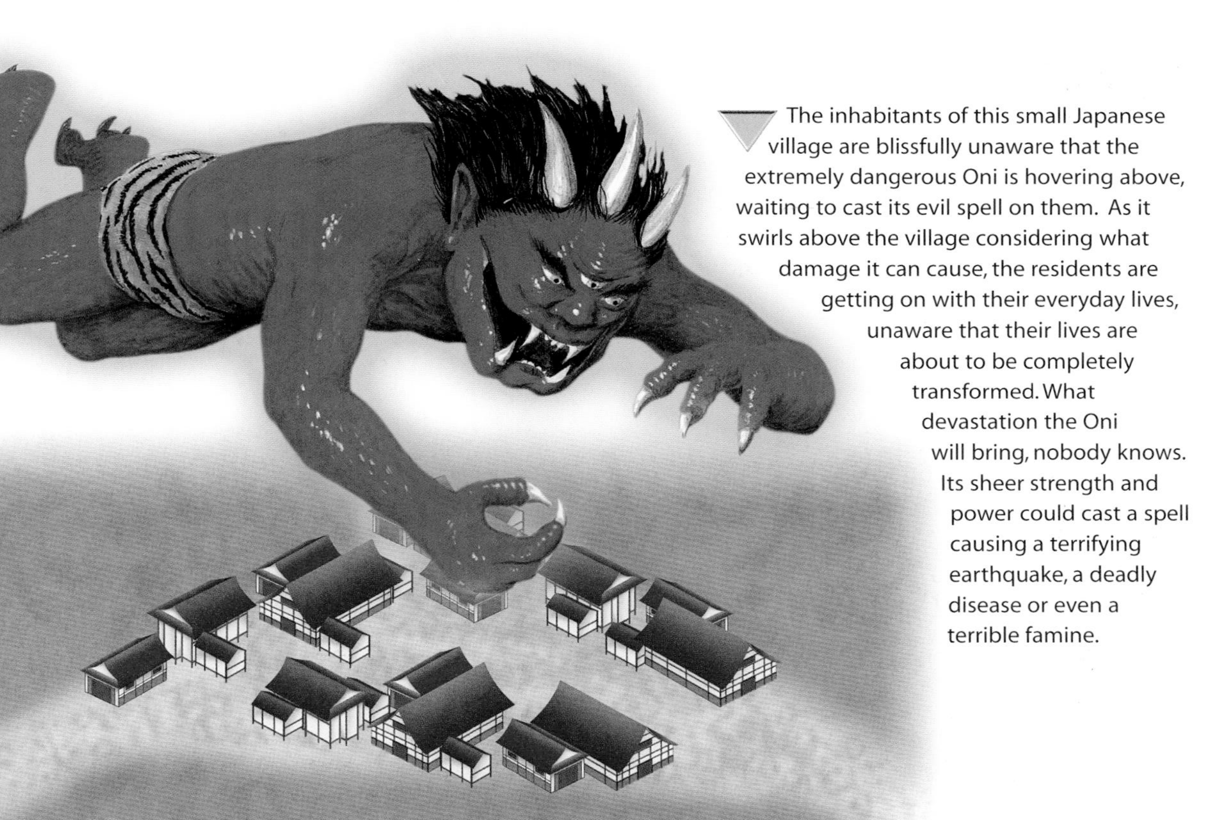

The inhabitants of this small Japanese village are blissfully unaware that the extremely dangerous Oni is hovering above, waiting to cast its evil spell on them. As it swirls above the village considering what damage it can cause, the residents are getting on with their everyday lives, unaware that their lives are about to be completely transformed. What devastation the Oni will bring, nobody knows. Its sheer strength and power could cast a spell causing a terrifying earthquake, a deadly disease or even a terrible famine.

WHERE IN THE WORLD?

Onis living in the mortal world are found almost exclusively in Japan, although they are thought to have originated in China. Other onis known as gaki inhabit the spirit world or Jigoku (hell) underground.

DID YOU KNOW?

- A woman may turn into an oni under the stress of jealousy or grief, while other onis may be the souls of people who died of plague or famine.
- The Buddhist sage Nichiren regarded the onis as a punishment for the sins of the Japanese, so he founded a school to reform people.
- Although female onis take the form of beautiful women, they are prone to violent outbursts of rage.

ROC

HUGE WINGS
According to the explorer Marco Polo, the roc has a wingspan of 48 ft (15 m) and feathers 24 ft (7 m) long.

FABULOUS PLUMAGE
In some stories, the roc is described as being bright white all over, just like its eggs.

SNARLING MOUTH
Hooked and pointed, the great bill is full of dagger-like teeth. The tongue is forked like a snake's, and laps up the last drops of a victim's blood.

EVIL EYES
Each bigger than a person's head, these can spot a victim from far away—when not keeping watch over the bird's enormous eggs.

VICIOUS CLAWS
The roc can pluck a 5-ton elephant from the ground with one claw, while a single slash from a talon can rip its belly wide open.

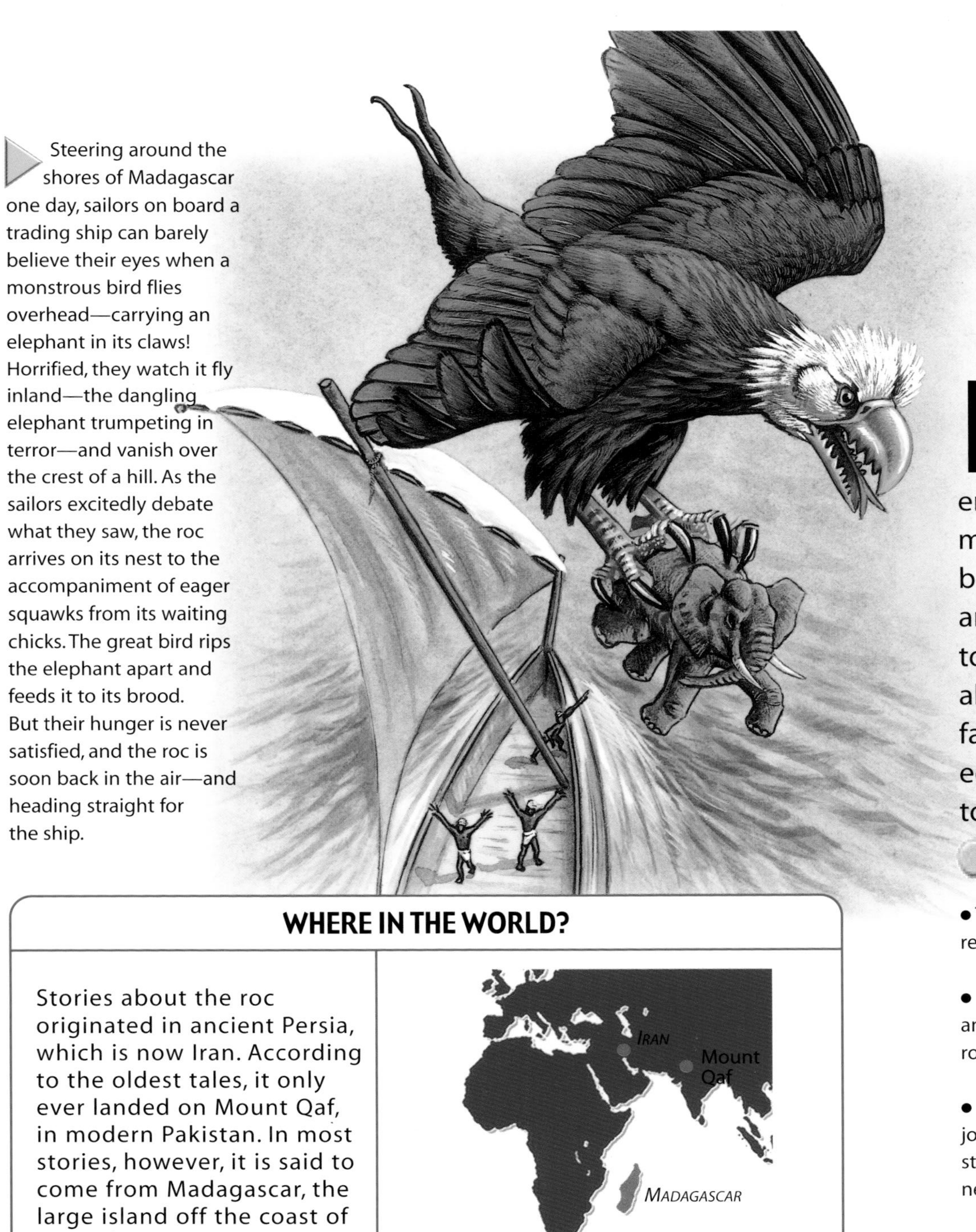

Steering around the shores of Madagascar one day, sailors on board a trading ship can barely believe their eyes when a monstrous bird flies overhead—carrying an elephant in its claws! Horrified, they watch it fly inland—the dangling elephant trumpeting in terror—and vanish over the crest of a hill. As the sailors excitedly debate what they saw, the roc arrives on its nest to the accompaniment of eager squawks from its waiting chicks. The great bird rips the elephant apart and feeds it to its brood. But their hunger is never satisfied, and the roc is soon back in the air—and heading straight for the ship.

Imagine a bird of prey the size of a large aircraft, with talons as big as sabers and a huge bill full of jagged teeth. The ancient Persians did, and called it the roc. It is a mythical beast of enormous size and strength, usually thought to live on the mysterious island of Madagascar. The roc is the ultimate storm-bird. When it appears overhead, day turns to night, thunder roars and lightning flashes. The beat of its wings causes terrible winds to sweep across the land and sea, sinking ships and devastating all in its path—even great trees and buildings. The roc nests in a fabulous jewel-filled valley, where it lays gigantic glowing white eggs. Terrified sailors are seized in its claws, torn to pieces and fed to the roc's young.

WHERE IN THE WORLD?

Stories about the roc originated in ancient Persia, which is now Iran. According to the oldest tales, it only ever landed on Mount Qaf, in modern Pakistan. In most stories, however, it is said to come from Madagascar, the large island off the coast of East Africa.

IRAN
Mount Qaf
MADAGASCAR

DID YOU KNOW?

- The roc—or rukh in Arabic—is thought to have inspired the rook in chess, a game which reached Europe from Persia in the 13th century.
- In one story in the famous book *The Arabian Nights' Entertainments*, Sinbad the Sailor's men anger a pair of rocs by breaking one of their eggs. The rocs retaliate by pelting them with rocks, sinking one of their ships.
- According to legend, merchants collected jewels from the valley of the roc by pushing huge joints of mutton off the surrounding hilltops. As the meat rolled into the valley, it became studded with jewels. Rocs then swooped on the mutton—but before they could take it to the nest, the merchants would harass them into dropping it at their feet.
- The roc was reputed to be so strong that it could carry off a rhinoceros and an elephant at the same time.

SCYLLA

NECK
A long, serpentine neck supported each of Scylla's horrible heads, enabling her to reach all the way from her underwater cavern to the ocean surface.

HEADS
Scylla's six heads were an indication of her origins, for though terribly distorted, they still retained some female features.

BODY
From the waist down Scylla had the body of a sea serpent—and in some tales, 12 misshapen feet were said to dangle uselessly from her scaly flanks.

WINGS
Sometimes, Scylla is pictured with wings, but rooted in her cave, she couldn't fly.

TEETH
Scylla was an avid flesh-eater, and easily tore flesh from bone with rows of shark-like teeth.

WAIST
At Scylla's waist, a girdle of ferocious dog's heads snapped and snarled at every passing ship.

▼ Circe tells Odysseus to steer close to the Italian shore as his ship enters the narrow Strait of Messina, and sails safely around the edge of the raging whirlpool Charybdis. But as soon as he reaches the far side, Scylla surges menacingly from her cave. Odysseus is powerless to stop an attack as Scylla's heads reach out and seize several of his best oarsman. All he can do is move on out of danger while the doomed sailors scream piteously.

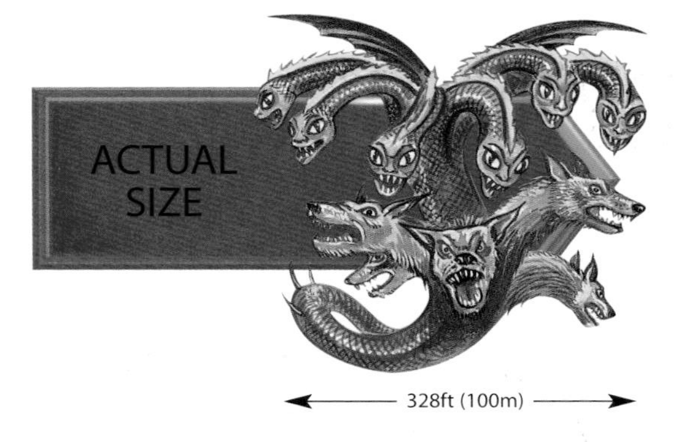

Sailors crossing the narrow strait between Italy and Sicily stood little chance of avoiding Scylla, with her awful shark-toothed jaws and belt of snarling dog-heads. She was featured in the epic poem *Odyssey* by the Greek writer Homer, and in *Metamorphoses* by the Roman poet Ovid. Once a beautiful maiden, she became a foul monster through the magic of the jealous sorceress Circe. She rose from the depths to devour sailors trying desperately to avoid the terrible whirlpool of Charybdis. Hundreds of sailors perished in Scylla's jaws, but her reign of terror ended when Hercules sailed through the strait. Hercules killed her with his club, but Scylla's father restored his wretched daughter's life, and she continued to haunt the strait.

WHERE IN THE WORLD?

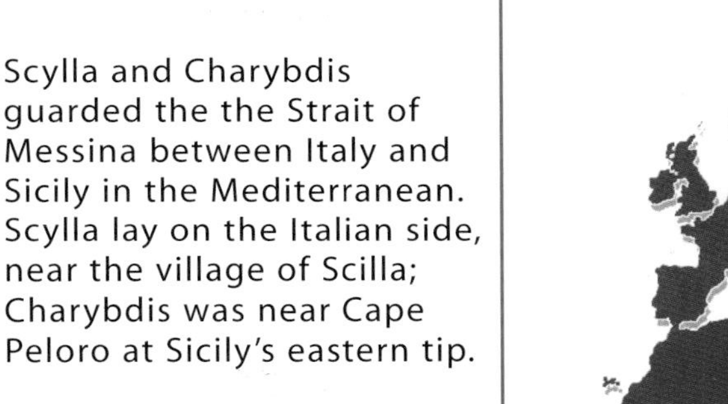

Scylla and Charybdis guarded the the Strait of Messina between Italy and Sicily in the Mediterranean. Scylla lay on the Italian side, near the village of Scilla; Charybdis was near Cape Peloro at Sicily's eastern tip.

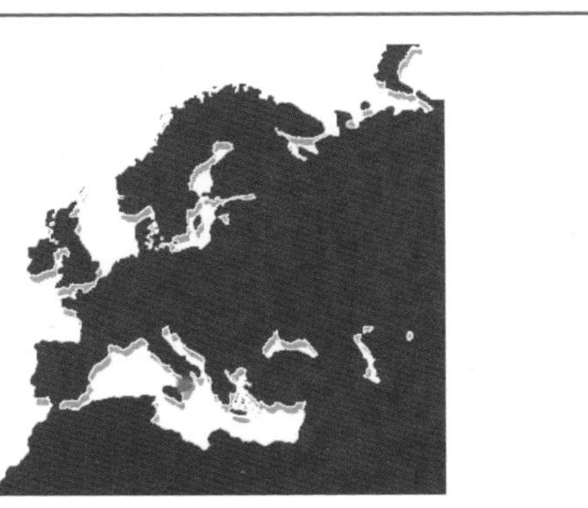

DID YOU KNOW?

- In some versions of the tale, Scylla is eventually turned into a rocky outcrop. This still stands today and is a real danger to passing ships.
- It's possible that Scylla and her snaking heads were based on sailors' tales of giant squid attacking boats.
- Whirlpools still occur in the Strait of Messina, and several historical accounts tell of large naval ships being sucked down to their doom.

SPHINX

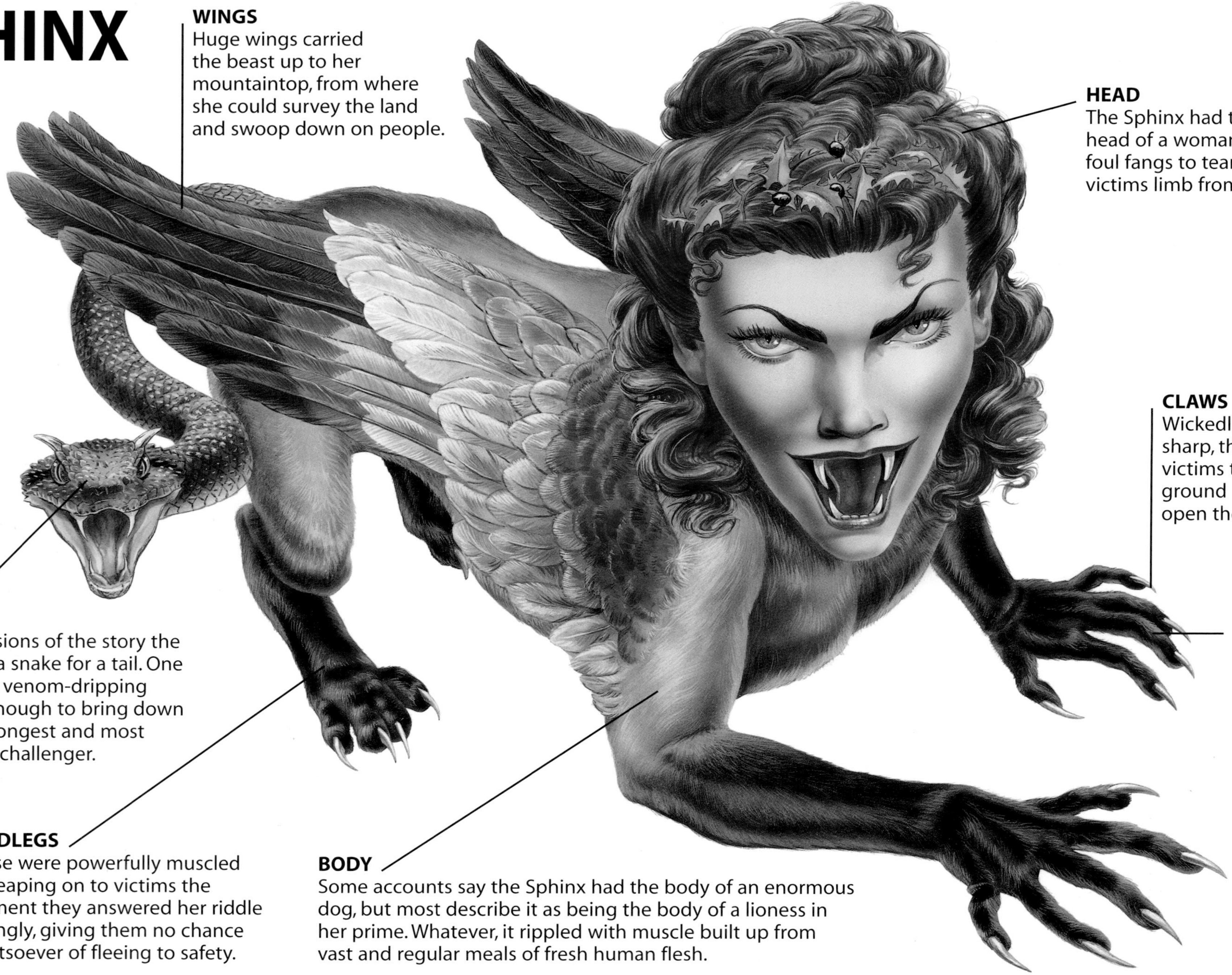

WINGS
Huge wings carried the beast up to her mountaintop, from where she could survey the land and swoop down on people.

HEAD
The Sphinx had the head of a woman, with foul fangs to tear her victims limb from limb.

CLAWS
Wickedly long and sharp, these pinned victims to the ground and ripped open their skin.

TAIL
In many versions of the story the Sphinx had a snake for a tail. One bite from its venom-dripping fangs was enough to bring down even the strongest and most determined challenger.

FOREPAWS
The Sphinx hel victims down with her huge clawed paws then crushed their windpipe with single massive bites.

HINDLEGS
These were powerfully muscled for leaping on to victims the moment they answered her riddle wrongly, giving them no chance whatsoever of fleeing to safety.

BODY
Some accounts say the Sphinx had the body of an enormous dog, but most describe it as being the body of a lioness in her prime. Whatever, it rippled with muscle built up from vast and regular meals of fresh human flesh.

High on Mount Phicium sits the Sphinx, guarding a narrow path. No one can pass unless they correctly answer her riddle—a puzzle taught to her by the Muses, the goddesses of the arts, and one she is sure no mortal man will ever figure out. Many brave men have tried: their bones litter the rocks around her den. Now, another intrepid traveler approaches. Nervously, he calls out: "Tell me your riddle, O mighty Sphinx." Fixing him with her steely gaze, the beast licks her lips then chants in a sing-song voice: "What walks with four legs in the morning, two at noon and three in the evening, and the more legs it has the weaker it be?" Trembling with fear, the man suggests "A grasshopper?" "WRONG!" screams the Sphinx and, before the man can escape, she pins him to the ground and clamps her teeth around his throat.

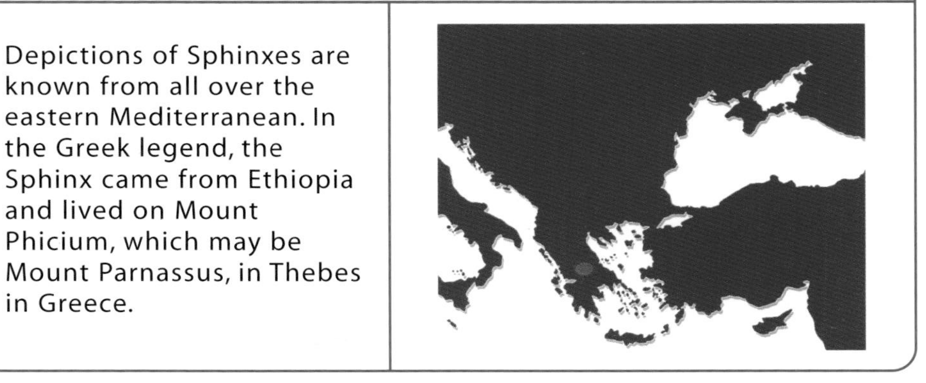

ACTUAL SIZE

This cruel monster of Greek legend challenged all who tried to pass her to solve a riddle—then slaughtered and devoured them when they got the answer wrong. The Sphinx was a horrible creature with the head of a woman, an eagle's wings, the body of a lioness and a snake for a tail, and she terrorized the poor people of Thebes in Greece from her domain on a mountaintop. She was finally killed by the Greek hero Oedipus, who marched straight up to the monster in her lair on Mount Phicium and demanded to hear her riddle. To her complete amazement, Oedipus answered confidently and correctly: "A man." Enraged, the Sphinx hurled herself off the mountain and fell screaming to her death in the valley below.

WHERE IN THE WORLD?

Depictions of Sphinxes are known from all over the eastern Mediterranean. In the Greek legend, the Sphinx came from Ethiopia and lived on Mount Phicium, which may be Mount Parnassus, in Thebes in Greece.

DID YOU KNOW?

- "Sphinx" means "strangler" and comes from the ancient Greek verb "sphingo," meaning "to throttle."
- Since it was carved over 4000 years ago, the Great Sphinx in Egypt has spent most of its time buried up to its neck in sand. The head has been badly worn by weathering and at some point lost its beard and nose. Also, troops of Emperor Napoléon Bonaparte (1769–1821) of France used it for target practice.

THUNDERBIRD

BACK
The thunderbird can carry an entire lake of water on its mighty back, releasing the water in torrential downpours.

EYES
Each time the thunderbird opens its eyes, bolts of lightning flash from the sky.

WINGS
Powerful wings with feathers as long as canoe paddles send claps of thunder echoing through the air.

HEADS
A second head sprouts from the thunderbird's chest, and both are equipped with viciously hooked beaks.

FEET
Huge, curved talons tip each toe, like those of a giant eagle or vulture.

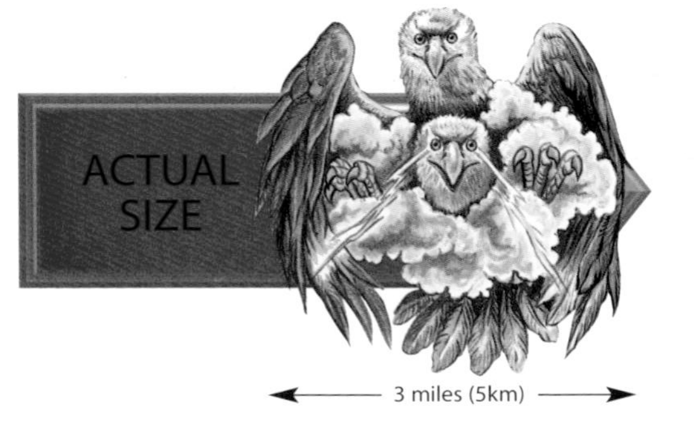

This gigantic two-headed bird-of-prey is known by Native American tribes to bring thunder and lightning to the skies. Lightning bolts shoot from its eyes, storm clouds are carried on its wings, and an entire lake of water on its back makes torrential downpours. Yet in Native American mythology, the thunderbird means different things to different tribes. Some tribes believe that the thunderbird is even the great creator spirit that made the heavens and the earth. Native tribes in Africa and Australia also have similar traditions to the thunderbird, no doubt inspired by the sight of eagles or vultures circling high up in the skies.

The Nootka people of Vancouver Island, off British Columbia, called the thunderbird Tootooch. To them, it was the sole survivor of four giant birds that preyed on whales (left, a sperm whale). By turning into a whale, the god Quawteaht tricked the birds into attacking him. He lured three to their death as he dived deep, but the survivor flew to the heavens. The story probably reflects the fact that storms often come from just one point on the compass. In the tales of the Quillayute people of the Olympic Peninsula in Washington State, the thunderbird and killer whale are deadly enemies. They once fought a fierce battle, shaking the mountains and uprooting trees as they struggled, creating vast treeless plains. Every time the thunderbird seized the whale in its talons, the whale managed to escape, finally retreating into the deep ocean.

WHERE IN THE WORLD?

Thunderbirds are part of the belief systems that were held by many different groups of Native Americans, from the Inuit peoples in the Arctic, to the Aztecs in Mexico. These gigantic birds are thought to live either in the sky or in remote mountain caves.

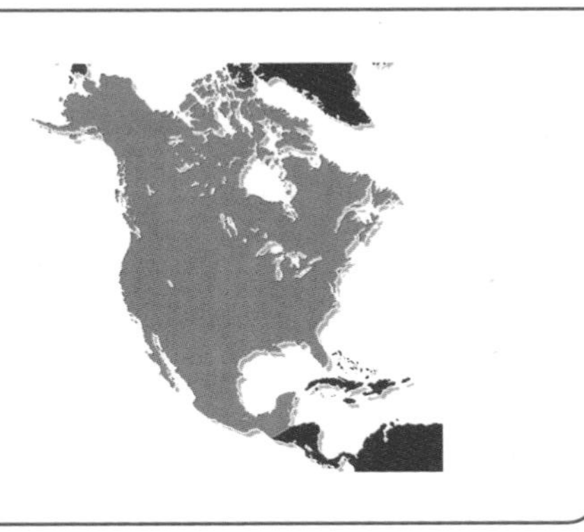

DID YOU KNOW?

- Many American tribes claim to have seen the thunderbird, and in South Dakota they believe it has left huge footprints. The prints are 25 miles (40km) apart in an area known as Thunder Tracks, near the source of St. Peter's River.

- Some stories say that the thunderbird lives in a mountain cave, burying its food in a dark hole in the ice. If hunters come too close, it rolls huge lumps of ice down the mountainside to scare them away.

WYVERN

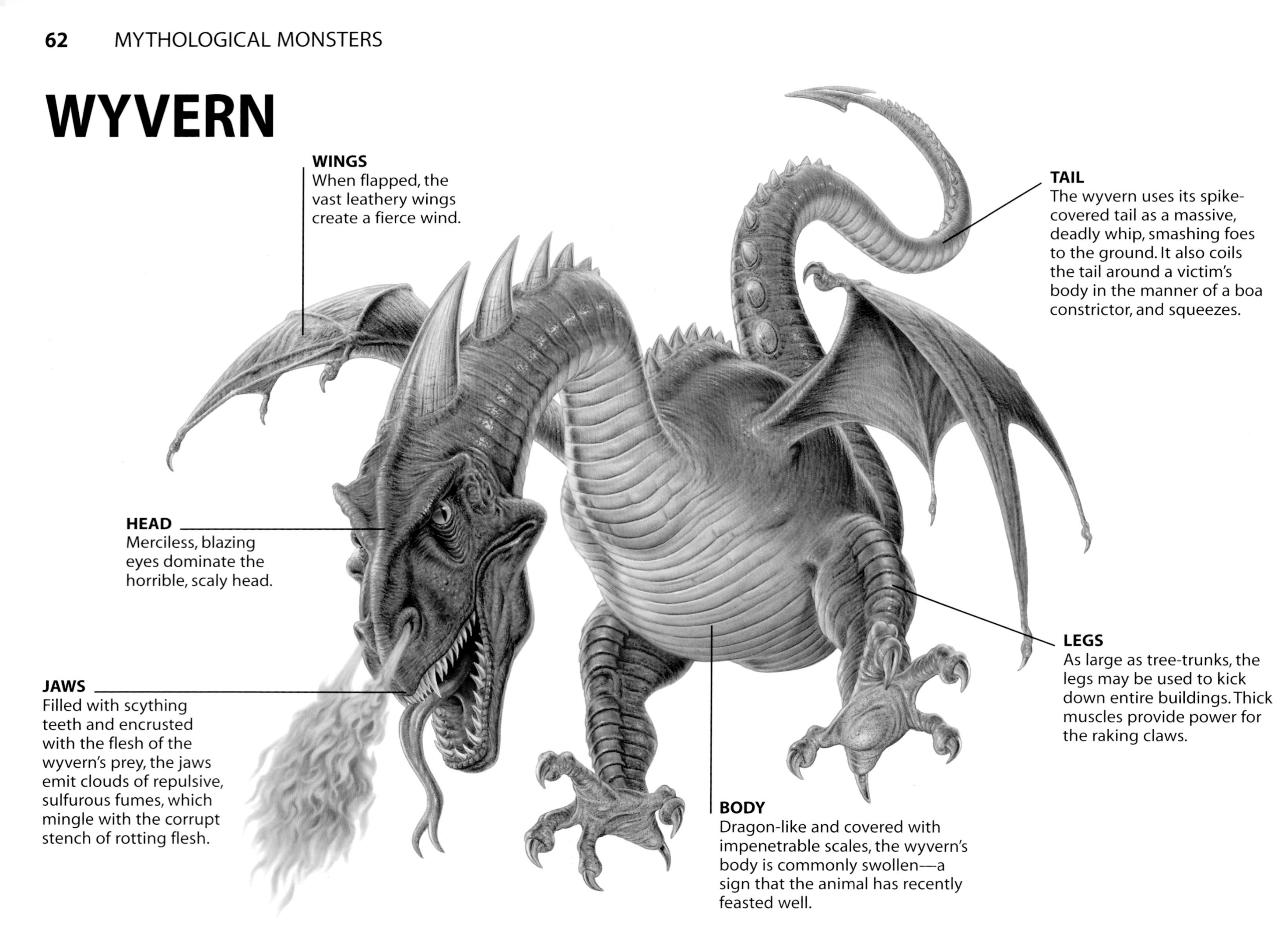
WINGS
When flapped, the vast leathery wings create a fierce wind.
TAIL
The wyvern uses its spike-covered tail as a massive, deadly whip, smashing foes to the ground. It also coils the tail around a victim's body in the manner of a boa constrictor, and squeezes.
HEAD
Merciless, blazing eyes dominate the horrible, scaly head.
LEGS
As large as tree-trunks, the legs may be used to kick down entire buildings. Thick muscles provide power for the raking claws.
JAWS
Filled with scything teeth and encrusted with the flesh of the wyvern's prey, the jaws emit clouds of repulsive, sulfurous fumes, which mingle with the corrupt stench of rotting flesh.
BODY
Dragon-like and covered with impenetrable scales, the wyvern's body is commonly swollen—a sign that the animal has recently feasted well.

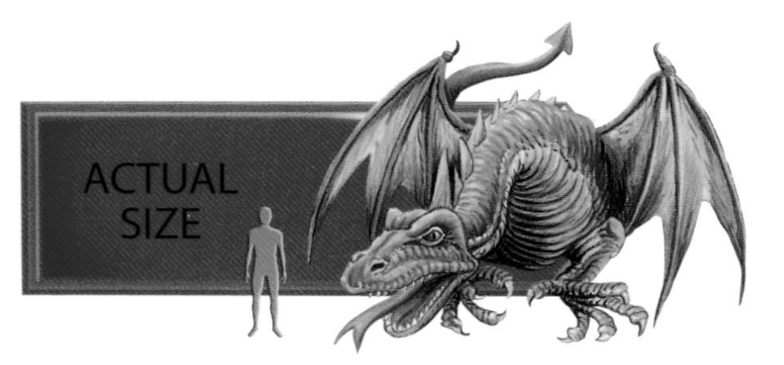

The dragon of medieval Europe, the wyvern is one of the most savage creatures ever imagined, with foul, scorching breath and fearsome fangs. It obliterates whole villages with one sweep of its spiked, serpent-like tail, and crushes victims in its scaly coils. The wyvern's mobility in the air, as well as its size and strength, makes it almost impossible to slay. In aerial attacks it kills with one sweep of its leathery wings, each the size of a ship's sail. The only way to defeat a wyvern is to fire a weapon into one of its two vulnerable spots: the "vent" just behind its legs or its open mouth.

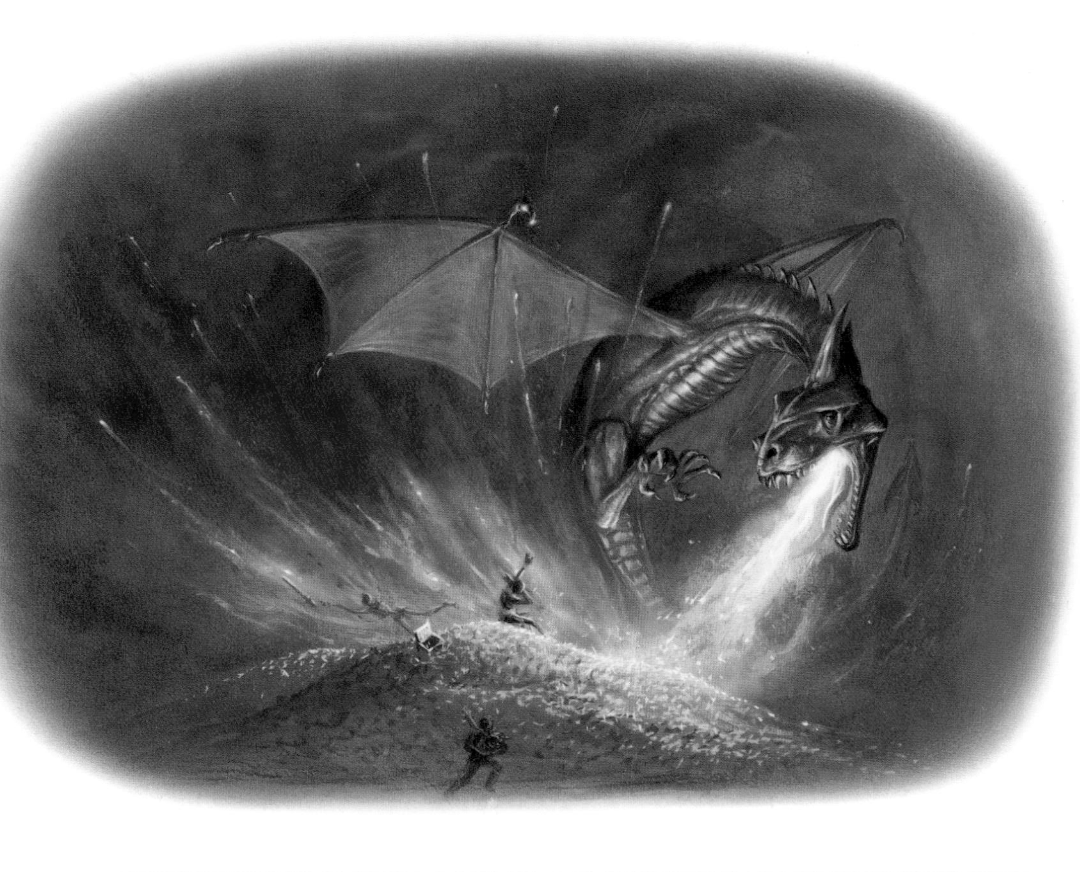

As a guardian of treasure, the wyvern has been the greatest challenge for many a legendary human adventurer. The foul beast's vast hoard of gold, silver and precious gems, gathered during a long career of terror and destruction, has lured dozens of greedy fortune-hunters to their deaths. To kill a wyvern and achieve greatness, a hero must be incredibly strong and brave—and lucky. Only after he or she is sure that the creature is dead can the battle-weary hero enjoy the spoils.

WHERE IN THE WORLD?

Dragons have been described by people the world over. Wyverns, however, are a particular feature of folk tales and myths from across northern Europe, particularly in Britain, France, Germany and Scandinavia.

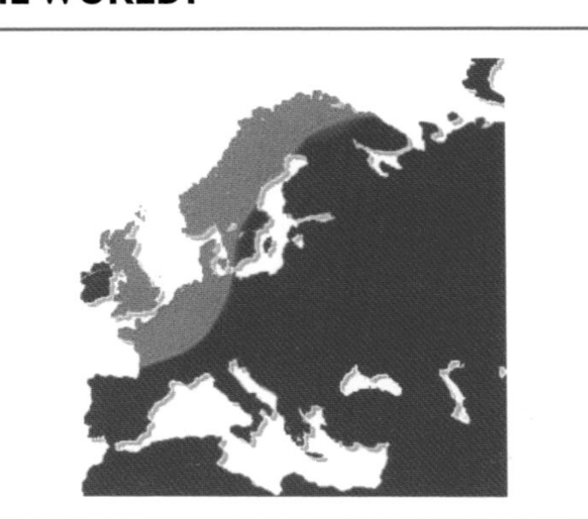

DID YOU KNOW?

- The name wyvern comes from the Saxon word "wivere," which means serpent. This word entered the French language as "wyvere" and came to mean viper.
- The wyvern was adopted as the symbol for the old English kingdom of Wessex.
- Like bulls, wyverns are traditionally enraged by the color red. In one Welsh myth, a dragon-slayer distracted a particularly malevolent wyvern by throwing a red rag into a river. The hero then shot the beast with an arrow.
- Up until the 16th century, people thought that fossil bones from prehistoric animals were dragon bones. In the town of Klagenfuhrt in Austria, 16th-century sculptors modeled the head of a statue of a local lindorm (wingless wyvern) on a skull found nearby. This skull was later discovered to be that of a prehistoric woolly rhino.

DRACULA

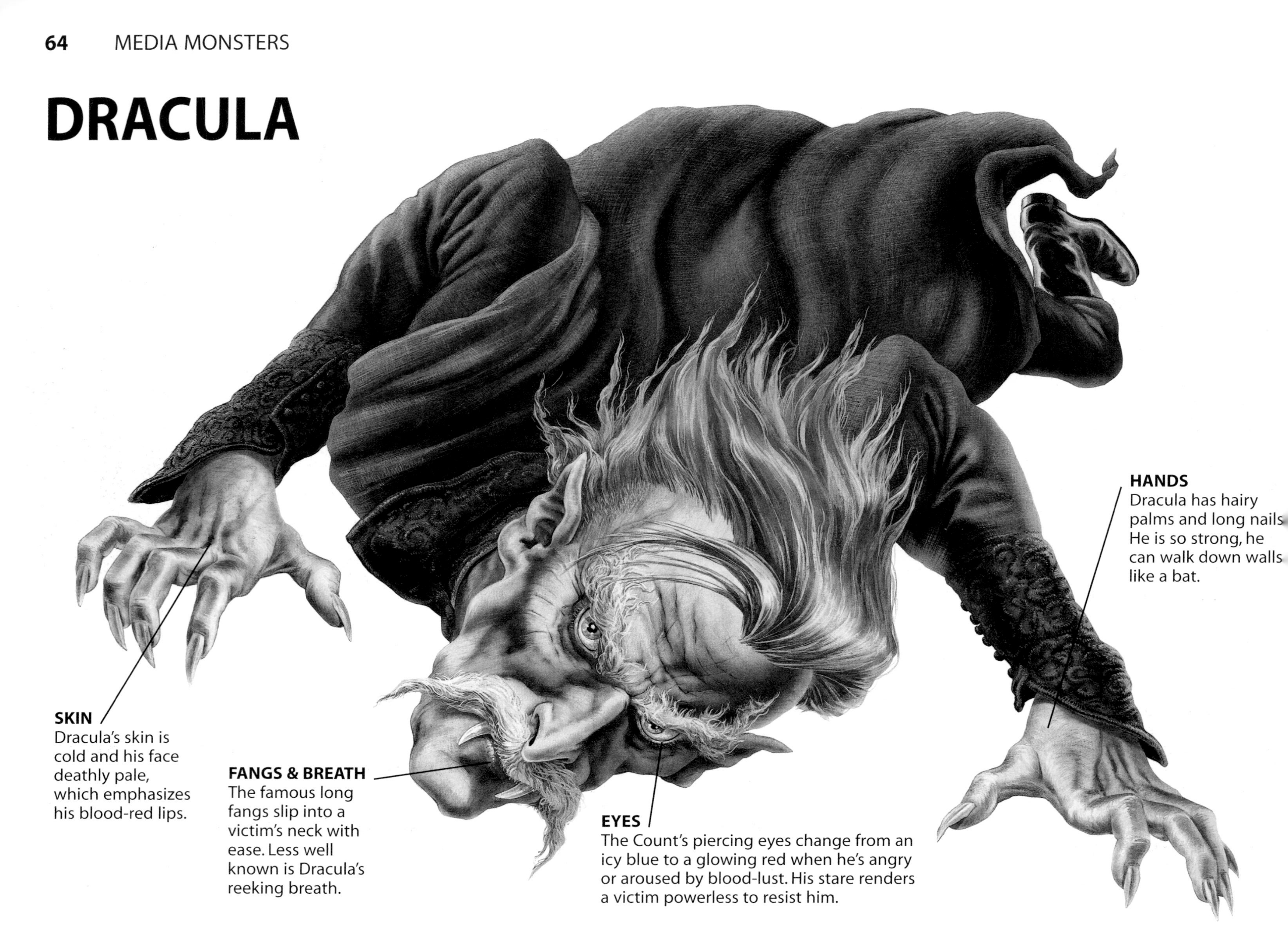

SKIN
Dracula's skin is cold and his face deathly pale, which emphasizes his blood-red lips.

FANGS & BREATH
The famous long fangs slip into a victim's neck with ease. Less well known is Dracula's reeking breath.

EYES
The Count's piercing eyes change from an icy blue to a glowing red when he's angry or aroused by blood-lust. His stare renders a victim powerless to resist him.

HANDS
Dracula has hairy palms and long nails. He is so strong, he can walk down walls like a bat.

Bram Stoker's dark tale ends with a brave team of vampire-hunters, including one Jonathan Harker and his friend Quincey Morris, chasing the Count from England back to Transylvania. Within sight of Dracula's castle, they finally catch up with the Count in his horse-drawn box just as night is falling. Harker and Morris burst past the vampire's helpers, hurl the the box from the cart and rip it open. The waking Count's eyes burn red with hate and triumph, but even as the sun sets and his powers return, Harker chops off his head and Morris plunges a knife deep into his heart. Within seconds, Dracula crumbles into dust. His evil rule is ended at last.

In his famous book *Dracula* (1897), Bram Stoker conjured up a true nightmare: a creature of the dark who feasts on human blood, infecting his victims with vampirism. Dracula was a centuries-old vampire, an "undead" being who drank people's blood to stay immortal—turning them into vampires, too. He lived in a remote castle high in the mountains of Transylvania in Romania, and had the power to change into a bat, a dog or a cloud of mist to carry out his foul deeds.

WHERE IN THE WORLD?

Dracula's ancestral home is a castle in the mountains of Transylvania in Romania. In the story, he sails to Whitby in northern England, moves on to London, then is chased back to his castle, where his reign of terror finally ends.

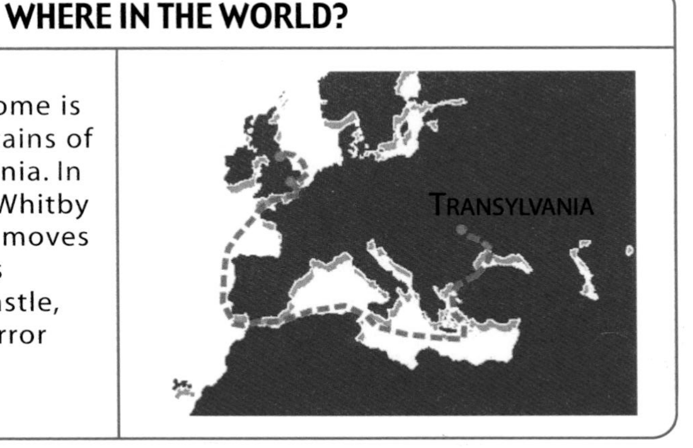

DID YOU KNOW?

- Bram Stoker was inspired to write *Dracula* by a disturbing dream in which a Count stops a beautiful young woman kissing his throat, saying "This man belongs to me".
- Stoker chose the name Dracula after reading about Vlad Dracula, a cruel ruler in Romania in the 15th century. "Dracula" means "devil" in a Romanian language.
- Vlad Dracula is also called Vlad the Impaler, as he impaled enemies on wooden stakes.

FRANKENSTEIN'S MONSTER

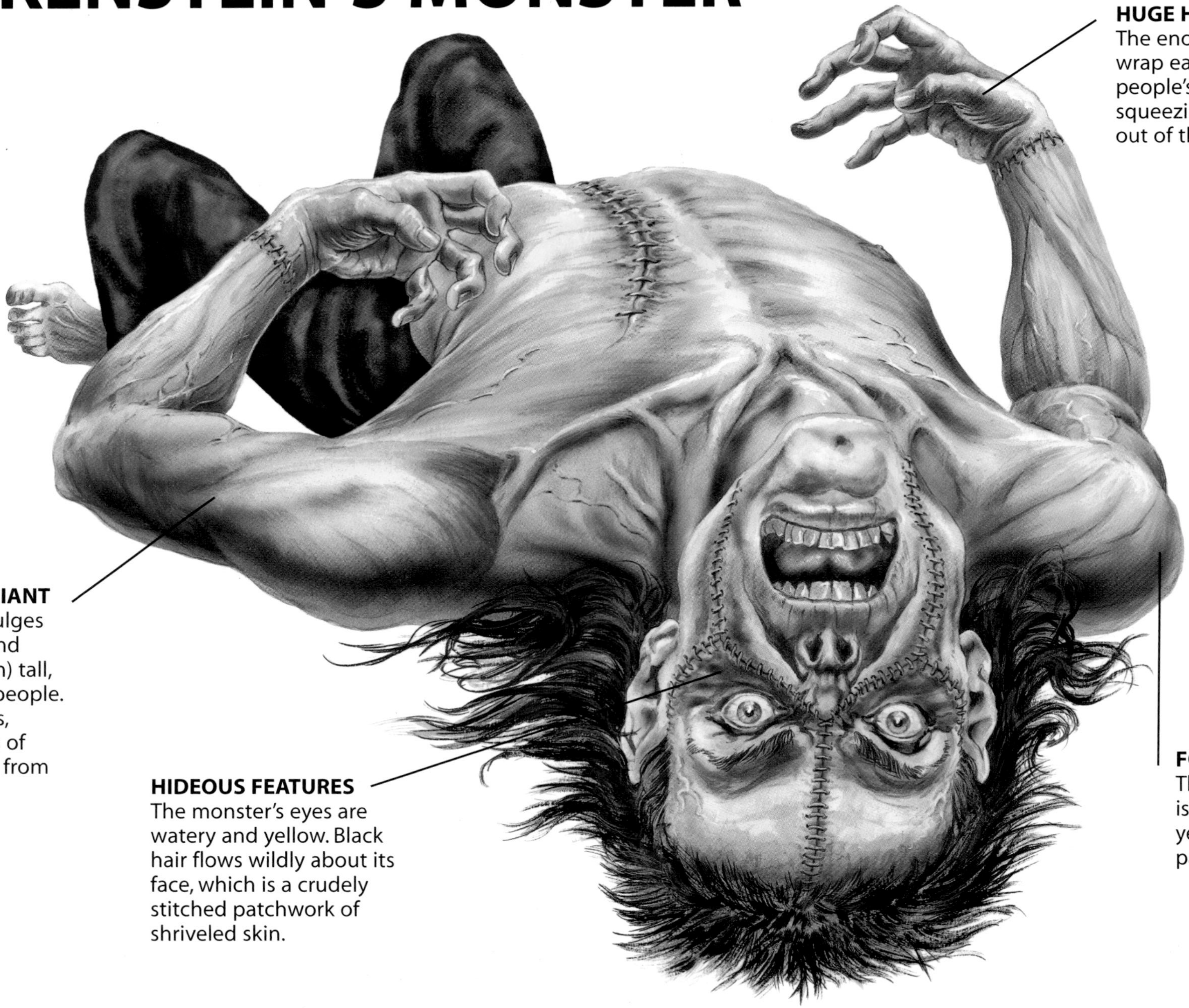

HUGE HANDS
The enormous hands wrap easily around people's necks, squeezing the life out of them.

GROTESQUE GIANT
The monster bulges with muscles and stands 8ft (2.5m) tall, towering over people. Head, legs, arms, torso—all parts of the body come from large corpses.

HIDEOUS FEATURES
The monster's eyes are watery and yellow. Black hair flows wildly about its face, which is a crudely stitched patchwork of shriveled skin.

FOUL SKIN
The monster's skin is taut, with the yellowish-gray pallor of corpses.

Frankenstein's evil monster is one of mankind's worst nightmares: a beast created by a mad scientist that wreaks murderous havoc on all around it. He is a giant creature sewn together from pieces of stolen bodies, brought mysteriously to life and endowed with superhuman strength. He then seeks revenge on the world when rejected by his creator, Victor Frankenstein. The monster was dreamed up one stormy night in 1816 by a young English woman, Mary Godwin (who became Mary Shelley).

WHERE IN THE WORLD?

Frankenstein created his monster in the town of Ingolstadt in southern Germany. The monster then follows its creator to the Alps, Britain and Geneva. Frankenstein then pursues it to the Mediterranean, the Black Sea and finally the Arctic Ocean.

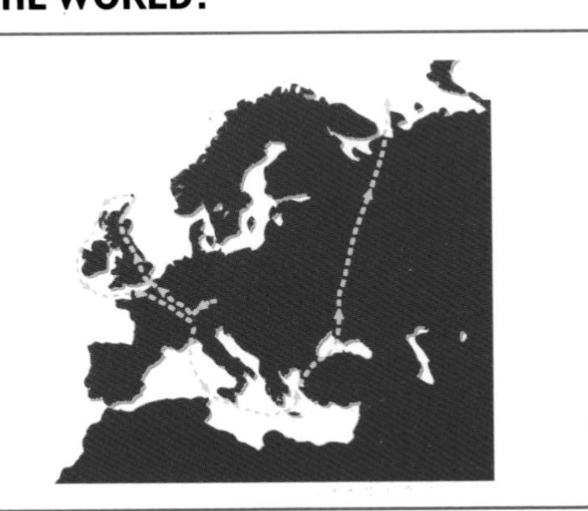

DID YOU KNOW?

- In 1831, Mary Shelley explained how the story of Frankenstein came about. In the summer of 1816 she was with Percy Shelley, the poet Lord Byron, Byron's mistress Clare Clairemont and his doctor, John Polidori, in Switzerland. The weather was bad one night and they couldn't go out, so they decided that each would write a horror story: the result was Mary's novel *Frankenstein*.

- *Frankenstein* was published in 1818—anonymously. Critics assumed that the author was a man and were outraged when they discovered that a woman had written the book.

- In telling her story, Mary Shelley was influenced by the discovery of galvanism. In 1791, Luigi Galvani, an Italian scientist, found that electricity made the legs of a dead frog twitch. Then, in 1803, his nephew Luigi Aldini passed electricity through the corpse of a murderer hanged only an hour earlier—sure enough, parts of the body began to move.

GARGANTUA

HEAD
Even before the age of two, his head was so big that each of his hats needed nearly 4843 sq ft (450 sq m) of fabric.

BELLY
Fat Gargantua was so heavy, he needed a horse the size of six elephants to carry him about.

HANDS
His pudgy fists could hold herds of cattle. The gloves he wore on cold days were made from the skins of 16 hobgoblins and trimmed with three werewolf pelts.

LEGS & FEET
Gargantua's stockings took over 5381 sq ft (500 sq m) of wool. The soles of his shoes were the stitched hides of 1100 brown cows.

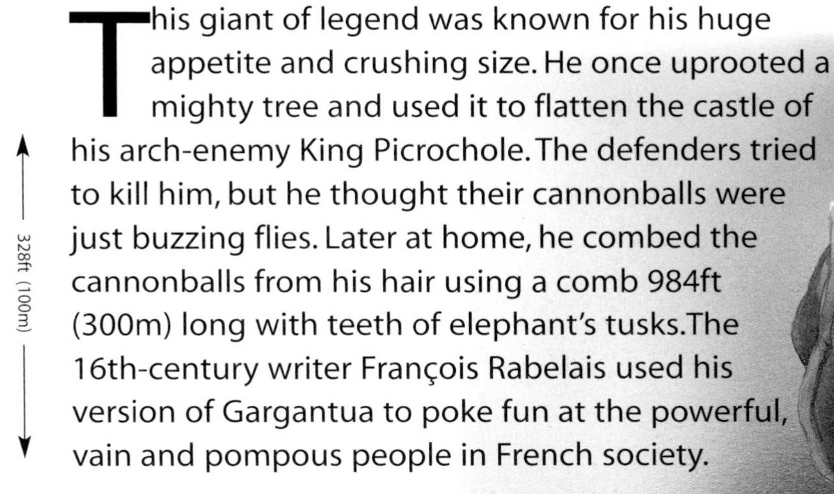

This giant of legend was known for his huge appetite and crushing size. He once uprooted a mighty tree and used it to flatten the castle of his arch-enemy King Picrochole. The defenders tried to kill him, but he thought their cannonballs were just buzzing flies. Later at home, he combed the cannonballs from his hair using a comb 984ft (300m) long with teeth of elephant's tusks. The 16th-century writer François Rabelais used his version of Gargantua to poke fun at the powerful, vain and pompous people in French society.

Six pilgrims find themselves without a roof over their heads at dusk. So they shelter in the vegetable garden of a great castle, hiding in some straw among giant cabbages and lettuces. For the castle is the home of Grandgousier, Gargantua's father. Feeling peckish, Gargantua grabs several lettuces in one hand, and with them five of the terrified pilgrims. He almost drowns them by seasoning them with oil and vinegar, then crams them into his mouth with the lettuces. The last pilgrim has hidden beneath a lettuce—but his staff sticks out, and Gargantua, believing it to be a snail's eyestalk, stuffs him into his mouth, too. Then one of the pilgrims, tapping with his staff before him, hits the nerve of a rotten tooth. Bawling in pain, Gargantua sends for a toothpick and loosens the pilgrims, who flee for their lives.

WHERE IN THE WORLD?

The legend of a giant named Gargantua may have come from Celtic tribes in Brittany, northern France, centuries before Rabelais wrote his book. Rabelais was born in Chinon, a town to the southwest of Paris. It was here that he set many of Gargantua's adventures.

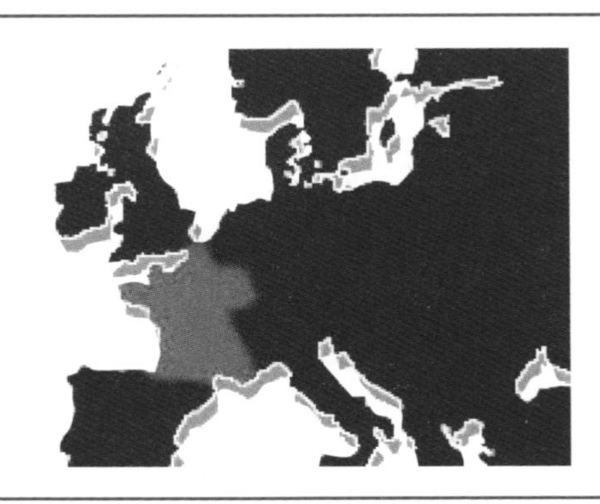

DID YOU KNOW?

- To this day, the word gargantuan means "huge", and it is often used to describe a massive appetite.
- The tallest person on record was Robert Wadlow of the USA. When last measured in 1940, shortly before his death at the age of 23, Wadlow was 8ft 11in (2.72m) high.
- Rabelais wrote that Gargantua fathered a son, Pantagruel, when he was no less than 524 years old!

GODZILLA

ARMS
These are used for punching and gripping. Godzilla often grabs hold of enemies and hurls them into the distance.

JAWS
The jaws contain ranks of metal-strong teeth, but also give out a radioactive beam that is lethal to humans and destructive to buildings.

LEGS
Using his mighty legs, Godzilla can run on land at speeds of up to 60mph (100km/h).

TAIL
The tail is not only a devastating spiny weapon, it is also used to propel the beast into the air for astounding jumps.

Godzilla was a remnant of the prehistoric age, a species of dinosaur known as the Godzillosaurus. Injured and awakened by US shelling during the Pacific War, the great beast mutated following later atomic bomb tests in the region, and grew to a height of over 300ft (91m). Then, turning upon the world that awoke him from prehistoric slumber, Godzilla unleashes a truly awesome destructive power. He is almost indestructible, with modern bullets and bombs bouncing off his armor-like hide. He also has weapons of his own, including (depending on the storyline) a lethal atomic energy beam that he fires from his vast and gaping jaws.

WHERE IN THE WORLD?

Godzilla has traveled the world in print and film, but his origins lie on the island of Lagos, near the Marshall Islands in the southern Pacific Ocean. It is a tropical region devastated during World War II.

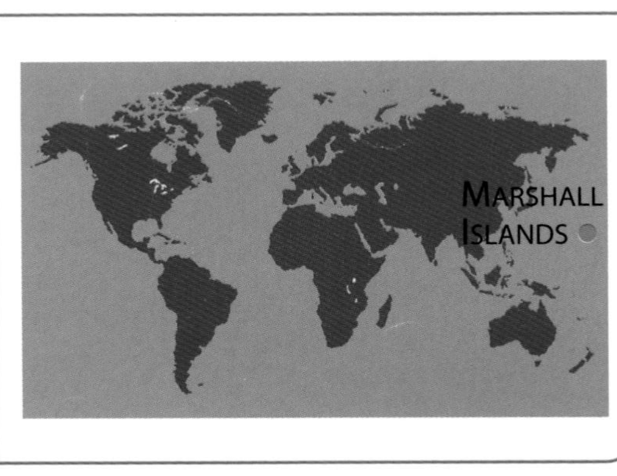

While swimming out at sea—where he moves underwater with the speed of a military submarine—Godzilla spots the sparkling lights of Tokyo on the horizon. He moves toward them, and the Tokyo citizens see his enormous bulk rise out of the harbor waters. Godzilla plunges into the heart of the city, smashing down entire skyscrapers with his tail and crushing cars, trucks and people under his massive feet. Having obliterated much of Tokyo's city center, Godzilla then slips back into the waters and disappears from sight.

DID YOU KNOW?

- Godzilla first appeared on movie screens in 1954, the film coming from the Japanese Toho Co. Ltd. His original name was "Gojira", but this changed to Godzilla to meet the needs of American audiences.
- Throughout his monstrous career in film and comicbooks, Godzilla has battled with numerous monster and alien enemies. His foes include King Kong, Mothra and Titanosaurus.
- "Gojira" combines the Japanese names for gorilla and whale.

KING KONG

BRAIN
Kong's brain is that of a massive predatory beast. Yet unlike many movie monsters, he also has some more caring emotions buried deep within.

BODY
At 50ft (15m) tall, Kong dwarfs any known primate, and is large enough to fight the prehistoric beasts that live on Skull Island.

HANDS
These are capable of crushing the life out of a human, but also of handling objects and people very gently when necessary.

ARMS
The enormous muscular arms can snap tree trunks in two and hurl cars through the air.

Having escaped from his chains of imprisonment on Broadway, the mighty Kong smashes through New York in anger, while also searching for his human love, Ann Darrow. He plucks Ann from a local hotel, and gently carries her across town in one hand—the other hand crushes trains, cars and buildings with horrifying ease. Finally, Kong ascends the Empire State Building, and places Ann on a ledge to fight off an attack by four US Navy biplanes. He manages to snatch one of the aircraft from the air, smashing it like matchwood. However, his end is near. Riddled by machine-gun bullets, he eventually dies and his enormous body plunges down into the streets below.

King Kong is the ultimate natural powerhouse, and a true movie legend. The first film bearing his name hit the screens in 1933, and he stunned audiences with his crunching aggression and also his unexpected tenderness. In the story, an American film crew encounter Kong on a mysterious island in the Pacific, known as Skull Island. They eventually capture the great beast, shipping it back to New York to display in Broadway shows. It escapes, and crashes through the New York jungle, finally ending it days atop the Empire State Building. Yet along the way, it also falls in love with a human, Ann Darrow.

WHERE IN THE WORLD?

Kong was captured on the remote "Skull Island" in the Pacific, a mysterious place inhabited by prehistoric beasts and violent tribespeople. From there he was transported by ship back to New York, where he is finally killed.

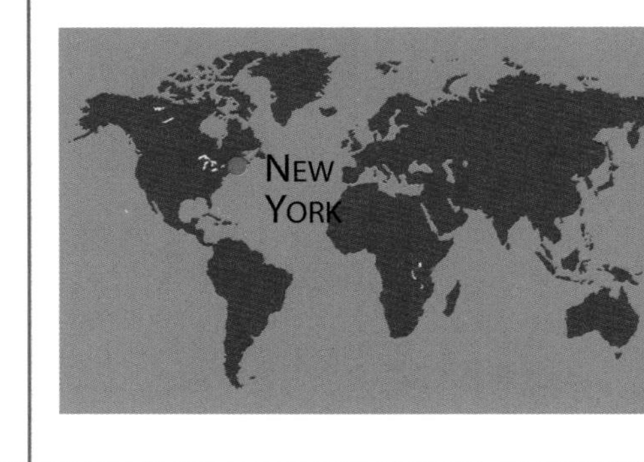

DID YOU KNOW?

- King Kong has appeared in numerous movies since his first appearance in 1933. These include the Japanese film *King Kong vs. Godzilla* in 1966 and the 2005 epic *King Kong*, directed by Peter Jackson who also directed the *Lord of the Rings* trilogy of films.
- The original *King Kong* movie amazed the audiences of the 1930s with the stunning special effects, which convincingly mixed real people with animated models.
- Kong has lost none of his popularity—the 2005 *King Kong* took over $50 million in its first weekend.

MOTHRA

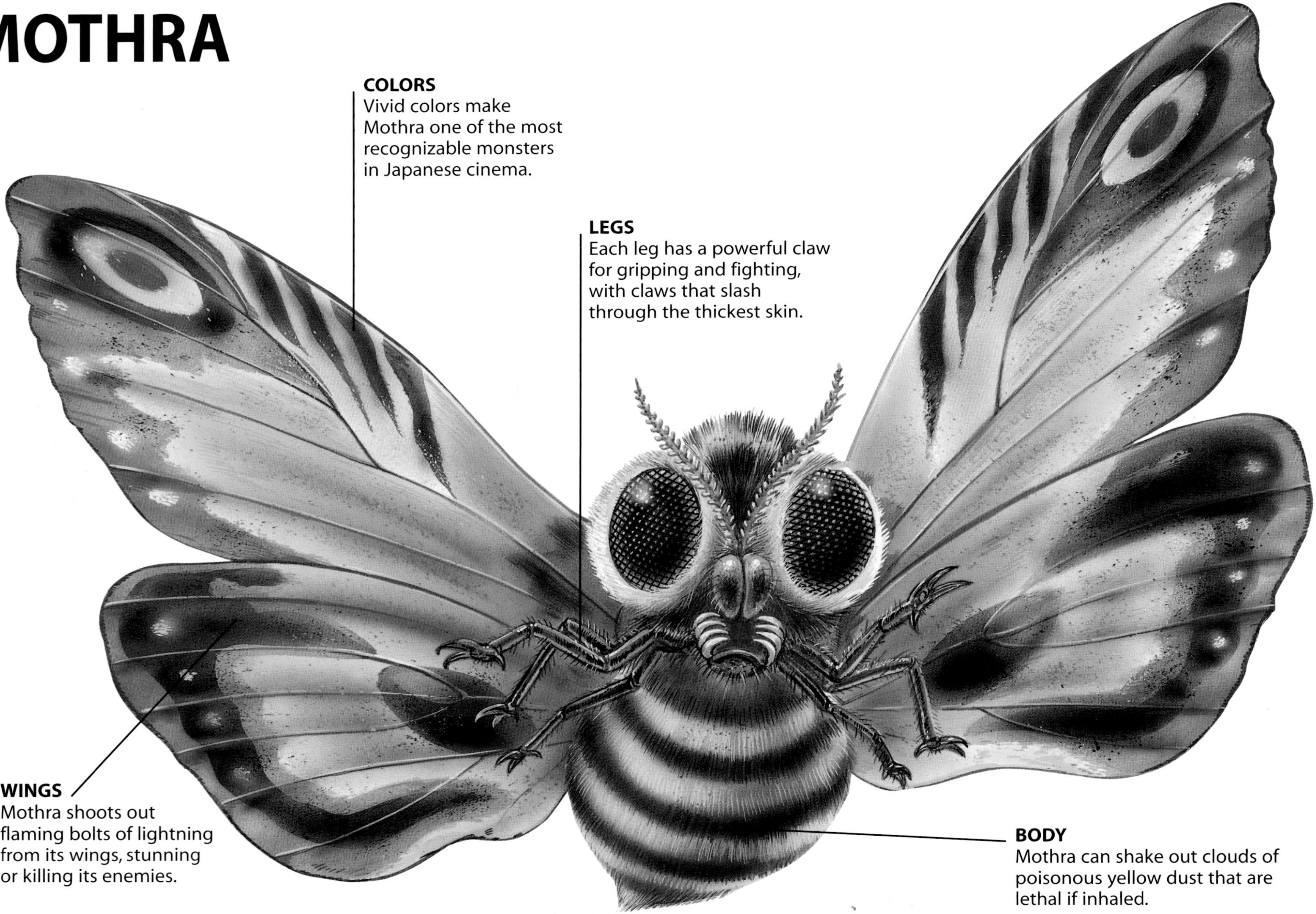

COLORS
Vivid colors make Mothra one of the most recognizable monsters in Japanese cinema.

LEGS
Each leg has a powerful claw for gripping and fighting, with claws that slash through the thickest skin.

WINGS
Mothra shoots out flaming bolts of lightning from its wings, stunning or killing its enemies.

BODY
Mothra can shake out clouds of poisonous yellow dust that are lethal if inhaled.

Mothra is an awe-inspiring and unusal modern monster. It is essentially a giant moth, and then some. Depending on the comicbook or film, this buzzing terror can grow up to 396ft (140m) long, and can weigh up to 15,000 tons. Its enormous wings enable it to fly at supersonic speeds, making it a challenge for even the most modern of military air forces. In spite of its appearance, Mothra is also highly intelligent, and it communicates telepathically with twin priestesses known as the Shobijin. Mothra has battled against several other monsters, including Godzilla.

Mothra, in all its astonishing colors, flies above a city holding its, ghastly offspring in its legs. The larva itself is a mighty creature—it has been recorded at lengths of up to 180m (590ft) and weighing up to 20,000 tons. Military helicopters circle the pair, but they will be left behind should Mothra decide to open its wings and speed off into the sky. Despite the threatening appearance of the scene, Mothra has come to the aid of humanity on several occasions, such as when it took on Godzilla.

WHERE IN THE WORLD?

Mothra is, like Godzilla, a Japanese creation, first introduced in Japanese film in 1961. It has battled with various monsters around the Japanese homeland.

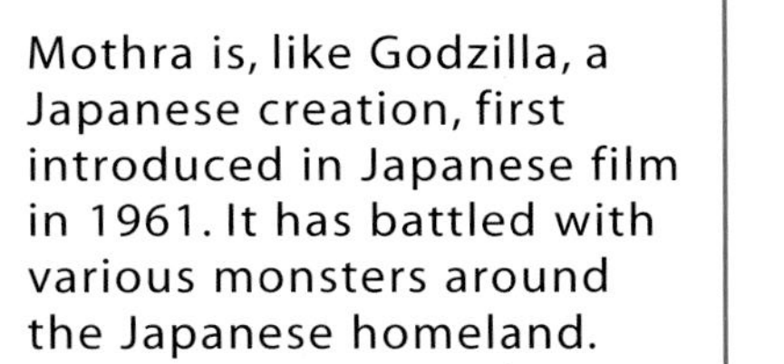

DID YOU KNOW?

- Mothra has been a popular recurrent figure of Japanese fantasy cinema. It appeared in as many as 14 title roles between 1961 and 2004.
- Mothra goes through the complete life cycle of a moth or butterfly. From a large blue egg, it hatches into a caterpillar, then disappears into a massive silk cocoon, from which it finally emerges as a fully grown Mothra.
- Mothra has numerous special weapons, including the ability to shoot bolts of lightning.

WEREWOLF

BODY
When the transformation is complete, the human body has turned into that of a wolf-like beast.

HAIR
Coarse hair coats the body. Some hair may remain even when the monster has reverted to human form.

EYES
Menacing eyes shine wildly in the moonlight.

TEETH
Large canine fangs and sharp cutting teeth easily sever flesh from bone.

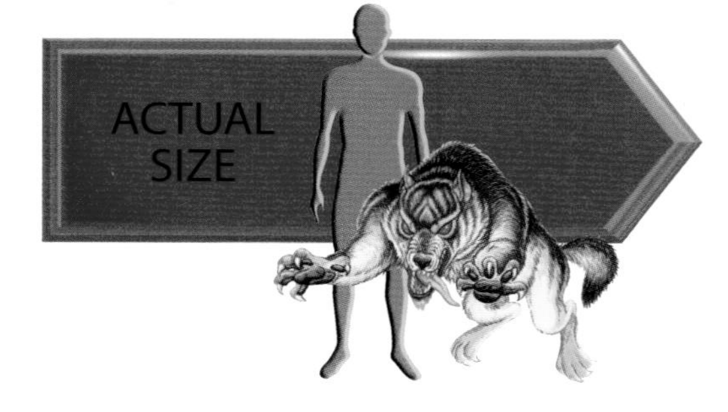

An innocent-looking human by day, a werewolf changes by night into a terrifying wolfish beast. It attacks victims with vicious claws and fangs, tearing the flesh from their bones, or digs up corpses from cemeteries to satisfy its ravenous hunger for human flesh. The belief in werewolves probably grew from the fear of wolves, whose ghostly howls could be heard through the night-time forests. Belief in werewolves was particularly strong in medieval Europe, and hundreds of innocent people were horribly executed by fearful mobs. Some really believed they were werewolves and confessed to their "crimes". In fact, they were suffering from a madness known as lycanthropy.

1 As the full moon rises into the sky and moonbeams strike his body, a man is racked with sudden pain: the curse has been activated.

2 A terrifying change takes place. His jaws stretch, his teeth enlarge into fangs, and hair breaks through his skin. He scrabbles wildly at his clothing with sharp, glinting claws.

3 By dawn, the werewolf has turned back into a man and lies exhausted in the cemetery, blissfully unaware of his earlier crimes.

DID YOU KNOW?

- In medieval Europe, people were regularly tried for being werewolves. One of the last convictions took place in 1720 in Salzburg, Austria.
- Many people believed that werewolves disguised themselves by hiding their hair inside their bodies. Suspects were often torn apart as prosecutors searched for evidence.
- Folk stories from around the world tell of people who change into tigers, leopards, hyenas and bears. Some even describe werepigs, which attack and bite passers-by.
- In European folklore, werewolves sometimes turn into vampires as they die, continuing their reign of terror.

WHERE IN THE WORLD?

Werewolf legends arose in many parts of Europe, Asia and North America inhabited by true wolves. The forests of France inspired the most stories: 30,000 cases were reported between 1520 and 1630.

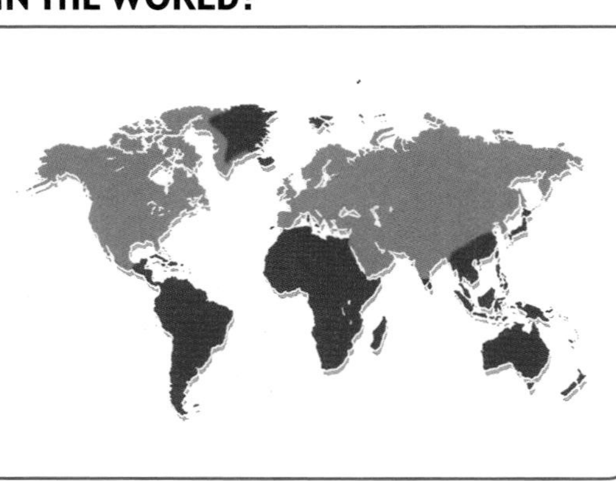

BIGFOOT

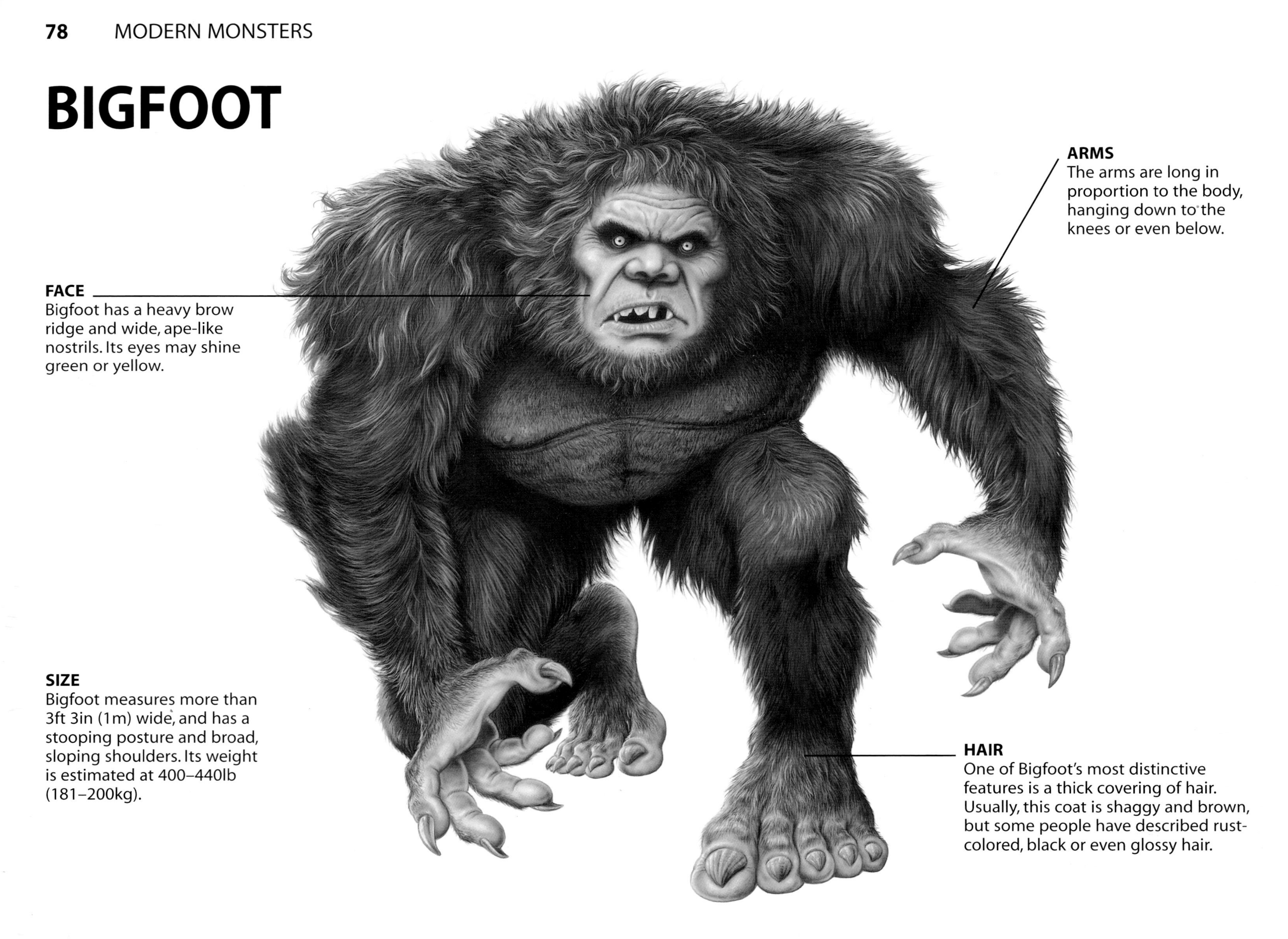

FACE
Bigfoot has a heavy brow ridge and wide, ape-like nostrils. Its eyes may shine green or yellow.

ARMS
The arms are long in proportion to the body, hanging down to the knees or even below.

SIZE
Bigfoot measures more than 3ft 3in (1m) wide, and has a stooping posture and broad, sloping shoulders. Its weight is estimated at 400–440lb (181–200kg).

HAIR
One of Bigfoot's most distinctive features is a thick covering of hair. Usually, this coat is shaggy and brown, but some people have described rust-colored, black or even glossy hair.

This terrifying, ape-like creature is said to roam in remote mountain forests, but it has eluded researchers and baffled sceptics for more than 150 years. Standing well over 6ft 6in (2m) high, with arms down to its knees, Bigfoot can easily carry away dogs and livestock. More than 1600 instances of Bigfoot sightings or trails have been recorded in the United States and Canada since the early 19th century.

GIGANTOPITHECUS
This giant ape was the largest primate ever to live on Earth. Fossils of two species have been found in India and China, dating from between one and nine million years ago. Scientists think the ape lived in open country, but they don't know if it walked upright.

YETI
Although there have been few actual sightings of the Himalayan abominable snowman, or Yeti, many people have come across its distinctive tracks. Some who have seen the Yeti describe a creature with pale or white hair, while others report a darker coat and a pointed head.

ALMA
This "wild man" of Central Asia is reputedly smaller than Bigfoot and less ape-like in build. In the late 1950s, based on his research into reported sightings, Soviet scientist Boris Porshnev suggested that these "wild men" were remnant populations of Neanderthal man.

WHERE IN THE WORLD?

More than 400 reports of Bigfoot sightings come from the west-coast American states of California, Oregon and Washington, and from the Canadian province of British Columbia. Other sightings have been reported from almost every part of Canada and the USA.

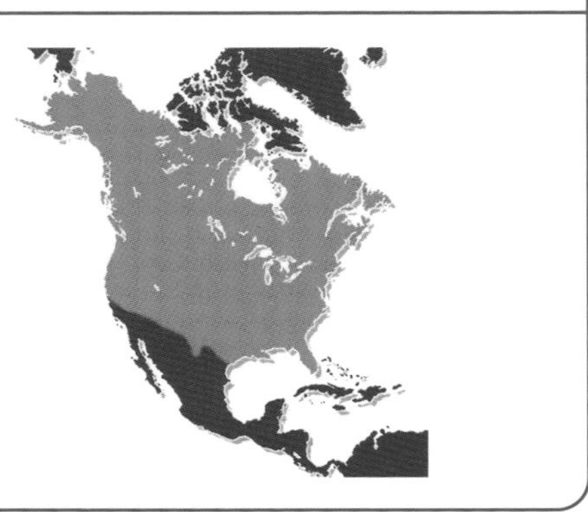

DID YOU KNOW?

- Many people who have shot at Bigfoot from point-blank range report that the creature seems invulnerable to gunfire.
- In 1995, a sample of alleged Bigfoot hair was sent for DNA analysis at Ohio State University. After years of testing, the results are still inconclusive.
- Hunters claim their dogs shy away from Bigfoot, whimpering.

GRAY ALIEN

HEAD
The huge, bulbous skull houses a massive brain, which gives the Grays their advanced technological abilities and telepathic powers.

EYES
Grays have huge, almond-shaped eyes, maybe to cope with low light levels on their home world.

FINGERS
Various reports say the Grays have from three to six fingers, possibly with suckers on the tips.

LIMBS
The legs are thin and weak with little muscle—perhaps on their home planet, Grays travel only by machine.

The mysterious gray aliens, or "Grays", are sinister beings from another planet that regularly visit our world in "flying saucers". They frequently kidnap people and perform bizarre medical experiments on them. The most famous incident involving Grays, the reported crash of a UFO on a small farm in Roswell, New Mexico, happened in July 1947. Initially the US military announced that they had recovered the wreckage of an alien spacecraft, along with the bodies of its occupants. Later, army officials denied this, but in 1995 someone produced what he claimed was film footage he had acquired showing the autopsy of two gray aliens recovered from the Roswell crash site.

Abducted from his bedroom after unearthly bright lights encircle his home, an unfortunate man awakes to find himself on the examination table of an alien spacecraft. Paralyzed by a strange drug administered by the Grays, he is powerless to move while his captors circle him. Mysterious and silent, the Grays do not talk as they go about their work. Instead, they pass messages to each other's minds by thought alone. Using a bizarre-looking piece of equipment, the Grays examine the helpless prisoner. Unless the Grays use their telepathic powers to block their victim's memory before they dump him outside his home, he will remember this terrifying and painful experience for as long as he lives.

WHERE IN THE WORLD?

Sightings of Grays are worldwide but the two most important sites are in the USA. Roswell, New Mexico, is where a UFO is said to have crashed, and Area 51, at Groom Dry Lake, Nevada, is a government base said to house recovered alien equipment.

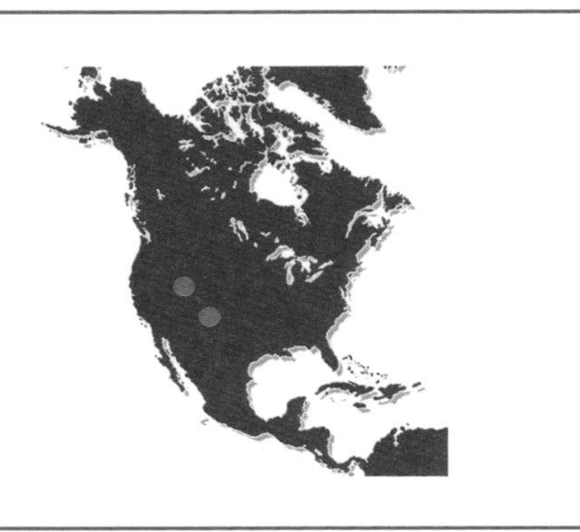

DID YOU KNOW?

- Abductees—people kidnapped by aliens—say Grays claim to come from a wide variety of locations in space. However, the majority of reports focus on Zeta I and Zeta II Reticuli—a star system some 37.5 light-years from Earth.

- Experts grade encounters with Grays and other aliens on a special scale from a "close encounter of the first kind", the sighting of a UFO, to a "close encounter of the fifth kind"—experiencing multiple contacts with aliens and their spacecraft.

- A nationwide survey revealed that about 5 percent of all people in the USA believe they have been abducted by aliens at some time.

HOPKINSVILLE GOBLIN

FACE
The monster has the merest bump of a nose, while its slit-like mouth is unnaturally wide and appears to have no lips at all.

SKIN
The smooth skin shimmers with a silver light that may be a protective force field, for it glows more brightly when the beast is attacked.

FINGERS
The bony fingers are tipped with curving talons like a bird of prey, and could inflict a serious amount of damage if the goblins ever decided to get nasty.

EARS
Don't try sneaking up on this little monster, for its bat-like ears can pinpoint the slightest sound.

EYES
Bulging on the sides of the head, the eyes burn brightly in the darkness, but are sensitive to too much light.

ARMS
Long and slender, the arms dangle almost to the ground when the creature stands upright, enabling it to drop easily to all fours so that it can gallop off into the safety of the undergrowth at speed.

BODY
Compared with humans, the being's slender body seems far too small for its head.

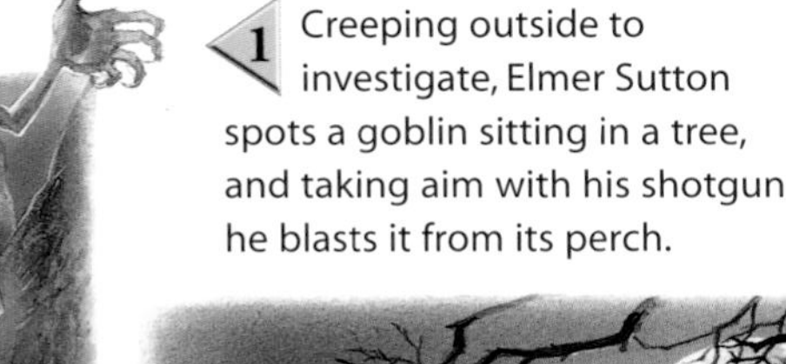

1 Creeping outside to investigate, Elmer Sutton spots a goblin sitting in a tree, and taking aim with his shotgun he blasts it from its perch.

2 But instead of tumbling to the ground, the eerie creature recovers in mid-air and floats toward its terrified attacker before scampering off into a bush.

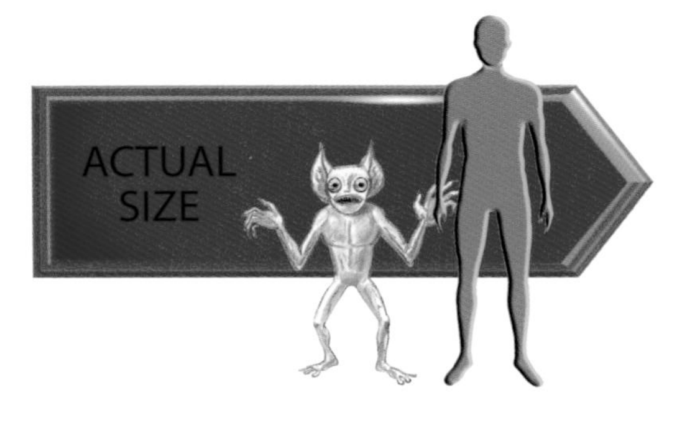

Alien or supernatural creature? No one knows the origin of the Hopkinsville Goblin, but Elmer Sutton saw one clearly enough to shoot it in a tree on his South Kentucky farm. Local Cherokee Indians also had traditions of visiting night time creatures that perfectly matched Sutton's description of what he saw. The case remains a mystery, but tales of goblins have featured in folklore since the earliest times. They are known as mischievous creatures, hiding out in underground grottoes, hollow tree-trunks or hidden areas around the house, emerging after dark to scare local humans. A few goblins are malevolent in nature, and have been known to get downright nasty.

WHERE IN THE WORLD?

The only documented sighting of the Hopkinsville Goblins occurred at the Sutton's farm near Kelly (sometimes known as Kelly Station), which is situated just north of the town of Hopkinsville, in south-western Kentucky, USA.

DID YOU KNOW?

- Investigators combed the area around the farm for clues, but the only signs of the encounter were stray bullet-holes, although one policeman did see a faint luminous patch on the grass where one of the goblins fell.

- Local Cherokee people tell of wide-eyed beings that shunned the light and had to be chased off when one of their tribes moved to a new hunting ground. So it seems that odd humanoids have appeared before.

JERSEY DEVIL

HORNS
Two goat-like horns top the creature's head, enhancing its devil-like appearance.

HEAD
The creature's head is similar to that of a donkey, but with a dog's nose and teeth. Its gums are rotten and its breath so foul that it curdles milk, blights crops and poisons rivers and lakes, killing fish.

WINGS
The leathery wings resemble those of a bat, and some say their span is surprisingly small, stretching to just 26in (65cm) when fully unfurled.

TAIL
Some say the whippy tail is tipped with a tuft, others that it ends with a three-pointed spike like that of the devil.

BODY
The body is that of a dog or horse. Though it's muscular, it's lithe in form for slipping down narrow chimneys, and emits a yellowish hue as the beast flies at night.

HINDLEGS
The Jersey Devil often walks upright on its two hindlegs, which some witnesses describe as being long and spindly like those of a crane.

FORELEGS
Each leg ends in a cloven hoof, but the forelegs are relatively short and stubby, and seldom used.

The bleak marshes of New Jersey in the USA have never welcomed people, and locals tell of strange sightings and chilling cries in the dark. According to many, something evil is out there. With bat-like wings and the head of a deformed horse, this inexplicable beast has been terrifying locals for more than 200 years. The devil emerges in the dead of night to haunt the countryside, killing wild and domestic animals and abducting small children. In January 1909, in a single week, more than 1000 people said they came face-to-face with the Jersey Devil, which appeared to householders, policemen and local officials. The accounts were all very similar, and local and national newspapers were forced to take the story seriously.

WHERE IN THE WORLD?

Many sightings of the Jersey Devil occur in the Pine Barrens of New Jersey: a lonely area of swamps and cedar forests covering 1698 sq miles (4400 sq km). But other reports come from all around the state, and occasionally from across the border.

Driven mad by hunger, the Jersey Devil leaves its dismal swampy home and flies to a nearby town, a glowing shadow in the night sky. After cruising over the rooftops, it spots a suitable chimney and dives swiftly down the soot-laden stack. The devil is unscathed by the fierce fire burning in the grate and bursts through the flames, scattering logs into the kitchen beyond. Screaming in terror at the nightmare vision, a maid watches in horror as the devil makes for the larder. She can only pray that the child upstairs remains silent—for a single cry might tempt the ravenous beast to sample fresher food…

DID YOU KNOW?

- In 1909, Philadelphia Zoo offered a $10,000 reward for the capture of the devil. This has prompted several hoaxes, including a painted kangaroo with a set of false wings. The reward remains to be claimed to this day.

- When the rotting corpse of a strange, devilish creature was found in the Pine Barrens in 1957, many people took this as evidence that the Jersey Devil was dead. But since then there have been several sightings.

LOCH NESS MONSTER

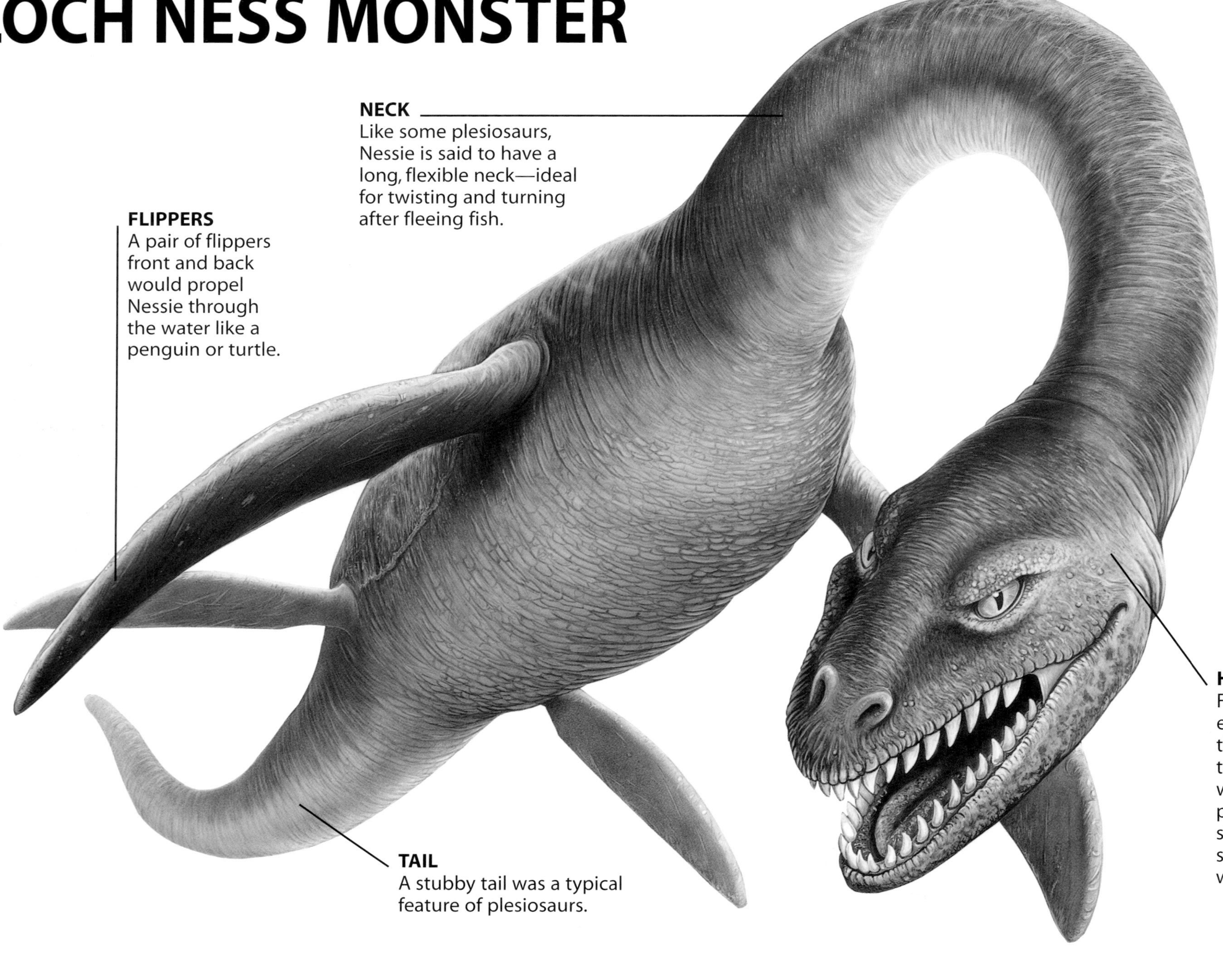

NECK
Like some plesiosaurs, Nessie is said to have a long, flexible neck—ideal for twisting and turning after fleeing fish.

FLIPPERS
A pair of flippers front and back would propel Nessie through the water like a penguin or turtle.

HEAD
Forward-pointing eyes would allow the monster to target fish. Nessie would also need plenty of needle-sharp teeth to seize slippery, wriggling prey.

TAIL
A stubby tail was a typical feature of plesiosaurs.

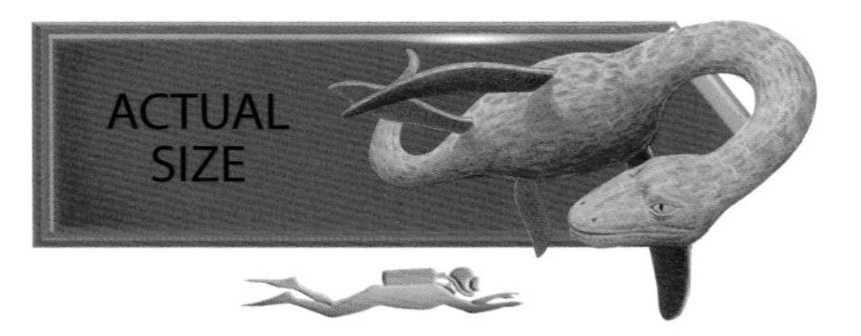

Legend has long had it that something strange lurks in the dark depths of Loch Ness—and since the 1930s, thousands of people have claimed to have seen a hump-backed, long-necked beast there. Some people claim that the "Loch Ness Monster" is actually a dinosaur whose species survives to this day in the cold Scottish waters. Other people say that the whole monster story is simply a myth invented by imaginative people. Whatever the reality, the fact remains that a number of people claim to have seen the monster. Even today the loch attracts tourists hoping to catch sight of "Nessie."

1 Some people believe Nessie is a prehistoric whale called Zeuglodon (or Basilosaurus), which is thought to have died out 18 million years ago. They say it lived at sea until after the last Ice Age then adapted to the fresh water of Loch Ness, where its blubber keeps it warm.

2 Enormous fish called sturgeon sometimes swim up the River Ness from the sea and enter Loch Ness in search of food or mates. Reaching several feet in length, with lines of prominent humps on their backs, they might explain many of the sightings of Nessie—especially when they are seen chasing salmon near the surface a long way out from the shore.

3 Loch Ness is home to brown trout, Arctic char, pike—and millions of European eels, which can grow to 6ft 6in (2m) in length. Many people who live near the loch believe the monster is nothing more than a large eel.

WHERE IN THE WORLD?

Loch Ness is part of a chain of lochs, rivers and canals in the Great Glen, a geological fault that runs right across the Scottish Highlands from the North Sea to the Atlantic Ocean. The River Ness links the loch to the North Sea.

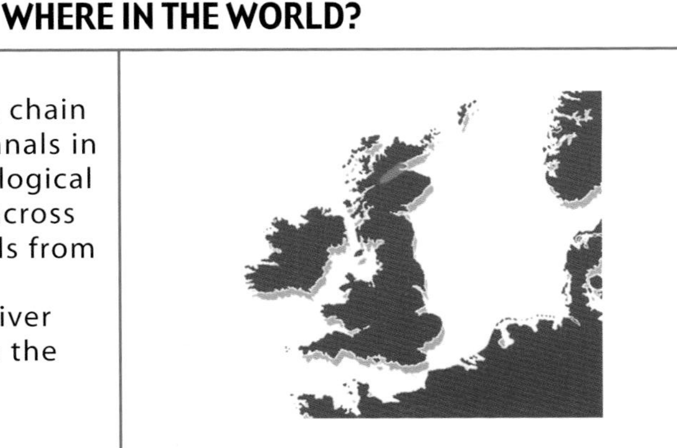

DID YOU KNOW?

- There is not a single recorded sighting of Nessie before 1930.
- A handful of claimed sightings have been on land, including one of the first, on 22 July 1933. A Mr. and Mrs. Spicer reported that a monster crossed the road in front of their car as they drove along the loch.
- Scientists who believe the Loch Ness monster exists have given it a Latin name: Nessitera rhombopteryx.

MOTHMAN

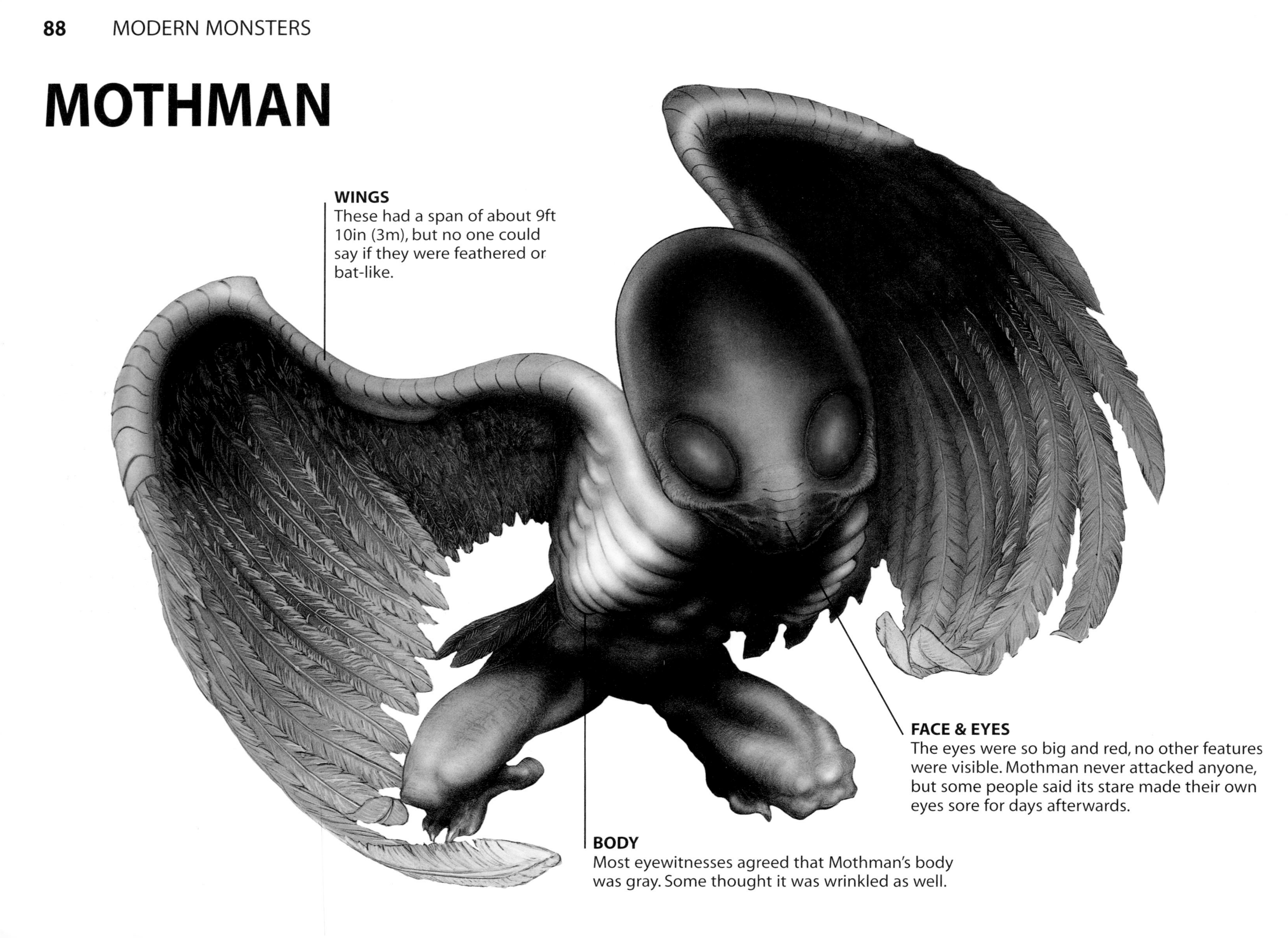

WINGS
These had a span of about 9ft 10in (3m), but no one could say if they were feathered or bat-like.

FACE & EYES
The eyes were so big and red, no other features were visible. Mothman never attacked anyone, but some people said its stare made their own eyes sore for days afterwards.

BODY
Most eyewitnesses agreed that Mothman's body was gray. Some thought it was wrinkled as well.

Its structure weakened by years of heavy traffic since its construction in 1928, the suspension bridge suddenly gives way, plunging cars and trucks into the icy black depths below. As the cries of people floundering desperately in the river fade, Mothman circles unseen overhead, calmly observing the terrible scene—then silently flies off into the night, never to be seen again.

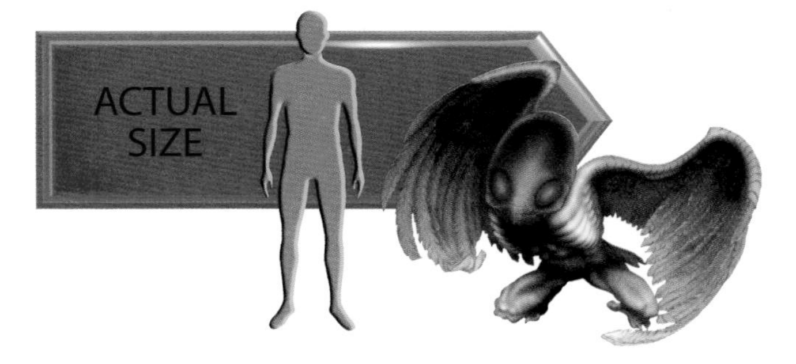

For 13 months in the mid-1960s, a bizarre "bird-man" with glowing red eyes haunted a small town in the USA. This winged being had a laser-like, hypnotic stare, and instilled utter dread in all those who saw it and was said to bring disaster. Witnesses to the monster described it as being taller than a man, and having gray skin, no arms and big wings, which it kept folded behind its back when on the ground. To take off, it unfolded its wings and shot up into the air, without flapping. One freezing night in December 1967, the Silver Bridge over the Ohio River in Point Pleasant collapsed at the height of the evening rush hour, killing dozens of people. To this day, monster-hunters blame Mothman.

WHERE IN THE WORLD?

Over 100 people claimed to see Mothman between November 1966 and December 1967 in and around the industrial town of Point Pleasant in West Virginia, USA. Most sightings were by young couples courting in their cars.

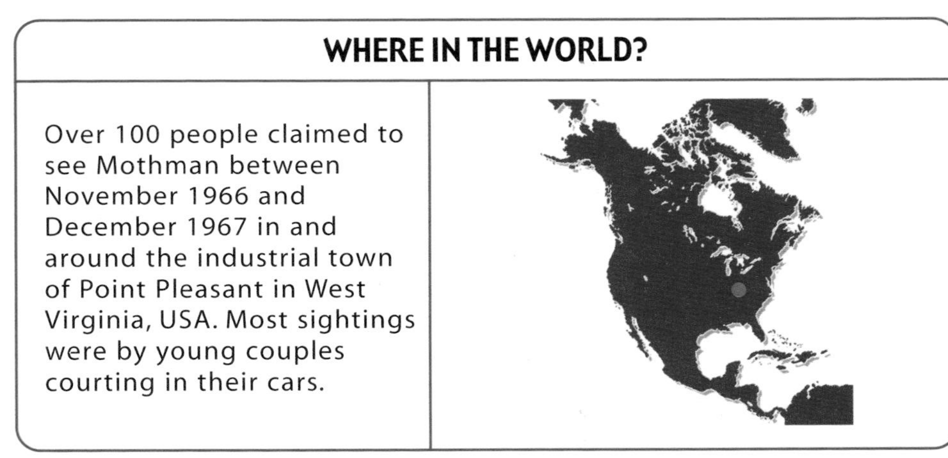

DID YOU KNOW?

- Mothman was first seen in Point Pleasant in 1961, by two people as they drove past a park called the Chief Cornstalk Hunting Ground—named after a Shawnee Indian who died fighting the British there in 1774. As he died, it's said, Cornstalk cursed the site for 200 years, a curse some people link to Mothman.
- A woman who saw Mothman was so frightened that she dropped her baby (who was unharmed).
- Many other countries have traditions of a bird-like creature that creates disaster.

REPTOID ALIEN

EYES
Huge and cat-like, these are probably sensitive to infrared light, enabling a Reptoid to detect its prey in the dark, by body heat.

MUSCLES
Despite spending long periods in space, a Reptoid is always powerfully muscled.

HANDS
These have just three fingers and an opposable thumb for gripping.

TONGUE
Just like reptiles, these aliens taste the air with a long, flicking forked tongue.

SKIN
Tough and scaly, this is adapted to withstand injury from the prolonged bouts of physical violence the Reptoids indulge in. Some witnesses also say that it glows with a lime-green aura.

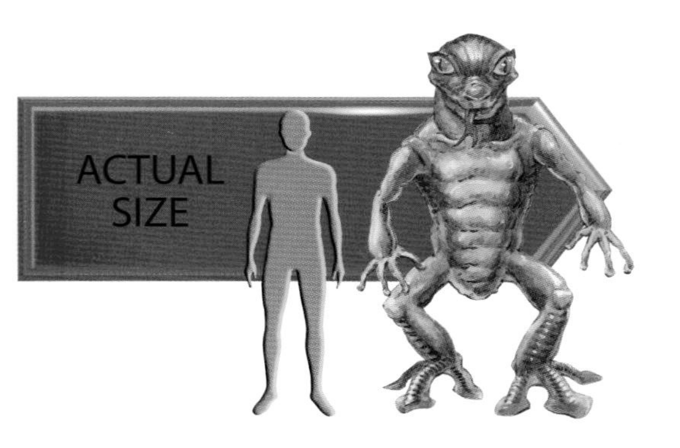

These scaly monsters seem to enjoy kidnapping both animals and human beings—so keep on eye on the skies. Some people claim they are aliens, while others think they are descendants of the dinosaurs. Whatever the case, they have supposedly left a trail of horribly mutilated animals across the United States. As well as being brutal and violent, the Reptoid alien is also highly intelligent. It is feared by some that one day they may take control of our planet, putting humans into the chains of slavery.

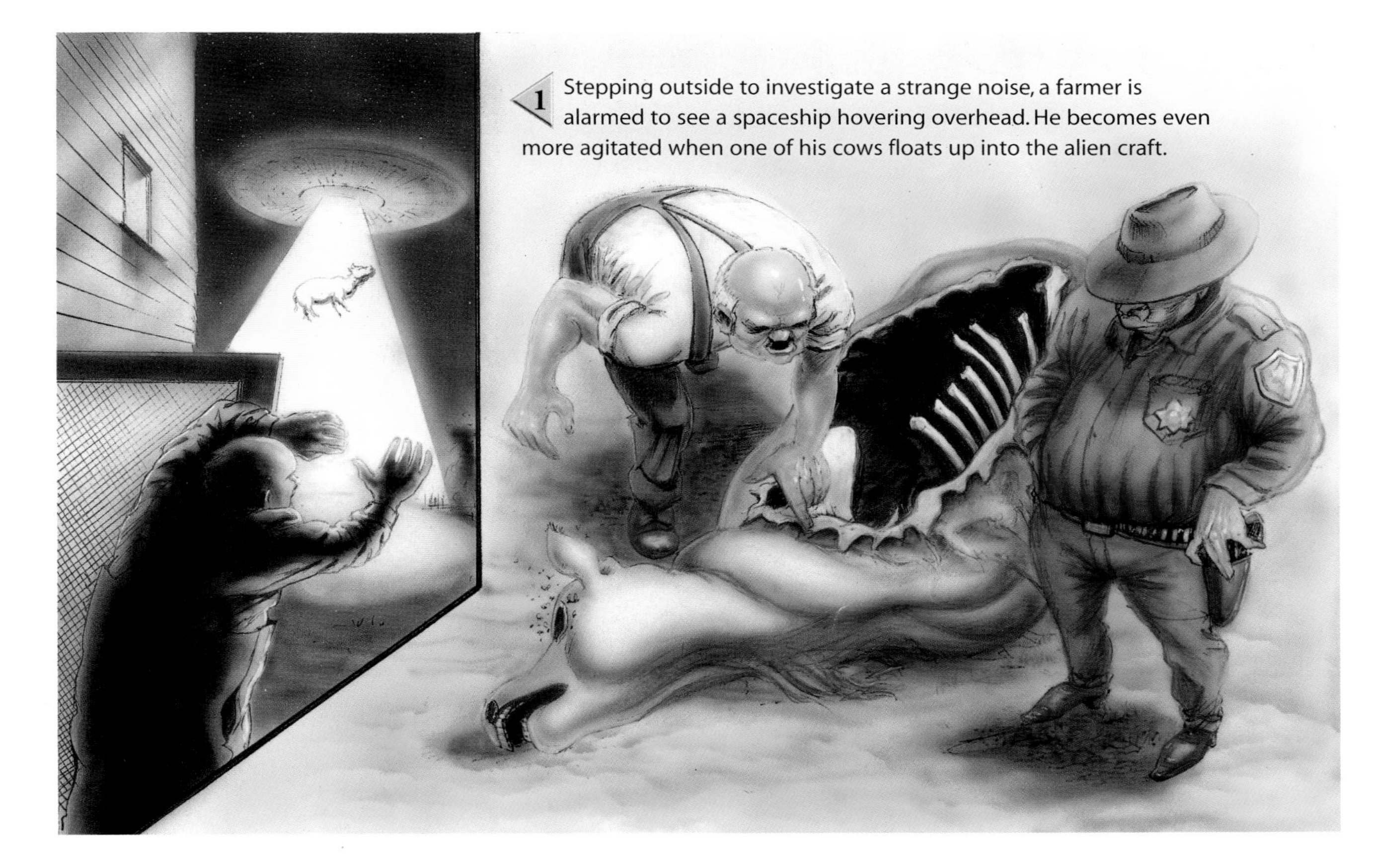

1 Stepping outside to investigate a strange noise, a farmer is alarmed to see a spaceship hovering overhead. He becomes even more agitated when one of his cows floats up into the alien craft.

2 Next day, he finds one of his cows drained of blood and with its eyes, tongue and innards surgically removed. But despite the evidence, the sheriff refuses to believe his story.

WHERE IN THE WORLD?

Reports of Reptoid aliens come from around the world, but these entities are most active in remote areas of the USA. Why the Reptoids favor these regions is unknown, but it seems they wish to operate without interference from the authorities.

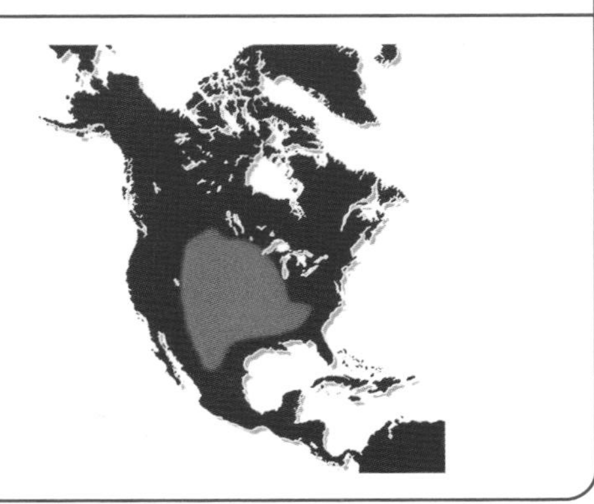

DID YOU KNOW?

- Some experts speculate that the Reptoids consider a cow's blood and organs a delicacy; others think they use the cows as an organic resource.
- Abductees say that the Reptoids come from the Draco star system.
- Some UFOlogists claim that the Reptoids avoid arousing suspicion by transporting their invasion force safely between stars in a massive spaceship disguised as a planet.

YETI

FUR
Thick fur protects the Yeti from the cold. In mountainous regions this is paler in color to blend with the snow, but on lower slopes the fur is a wiry reddish-brown.

MUSCLES
Witnesses report that the monster is strong enough to uproot trees and hurl boulders around.

LEGS
The Yeti walks upright with long, loping strides, leaving tracks that that are far too wide apart to belong to any known primate.

ARMS
The Yeti's arms are extremely long, hanging all the way down to its knees.

HANDS
It's never wise to get too close to a Yeti, because it could pick you up with one huge hand.

FEET
Shaped remarkably like those of a human, the broad feet prevent the Yeti from sinking too deeply into the snow.

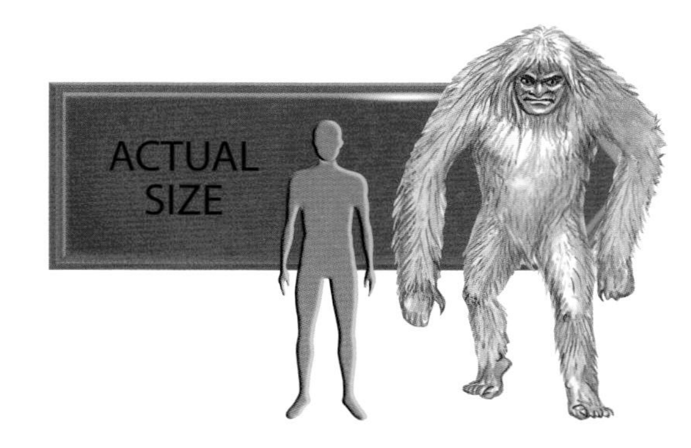

Tantalizing trails of oversized footprints are often the only indication of this hairy creature's presence as it wanders across the isolated slopes of the Himalayas. Both native Sherpas and foreign explorers have glimpsed this huge, upright figure loping across the snow. The Sherpas keep a close eye on the ground, and if they spot one of the Yeti's giant footprints, they will quickly get out of the area. Yetis are territorial creatures, and are said to kill and eat those who wander into their territories. Local traditions describe three different types of Yeti, the largest growing up to 15ft (4.5m) tall.

WHERE IN THE WORLD?

The Yeti is found in the Himalayan mountain range in Asia, with most sightings occurring in Nepal, Bhutan and Tibet. But some enthusiasts have also linked the Yeti with reports of similar-looking creatures such as the North American monster, Bigfoot.

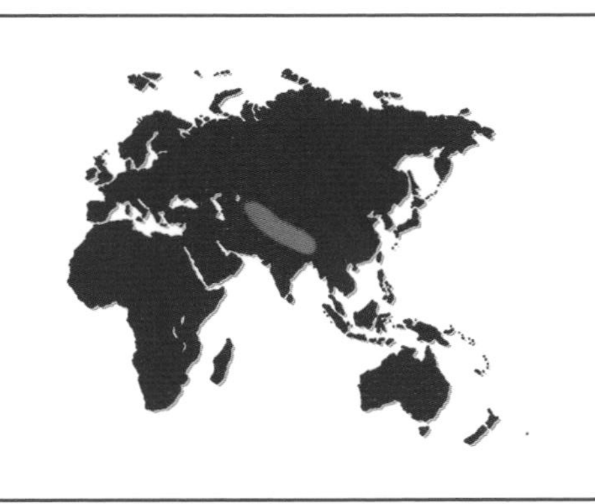

Lost in the heights of the Himalayan mountains, a lone mountaineer tries desperately to find his way back to civilization. But as he wanders blindly through the snow, he stumbles into the path of a huge Yeti. Howling with rage, the hairy beast rushes over and grabs the climber by the arm, incensed that a stranger has blundered into its territory. Then, striding onto a ledge, the monster dangles the unfortunate victim over a cliff with one strong arm, before dropping the climber to his death on the rocks far below.

DID YOU KNOW?

- In 1961, the Nepalese government officially declared that Yetis existed. It subsequently granted US $10,000 licences to any hunters dedicated and rich enough to stalk the beast through its Himalayan home.
- According to Sherpas, the Yeti is partial to a drop or two of alcohol.
- The best way to escape from a Yeti is by running downhill. Any Yeti attempting to follow will be blinded by the immense tangle of hair falling into its face and covering its eyes.
- Some people think the Yeti has transparent second eyelids, which protect its eyes during blizzards.
- The name "Yeti" is a Tibetan word meaning magical creature, but the Nepalese also know the beast as "Rakshas," the demon. The Chinese and Soviets call it the "Alma," while another Tibetan word for the beast, "Metoh-Kangmi," is often translated as the "abominable snowman."

YOWIE

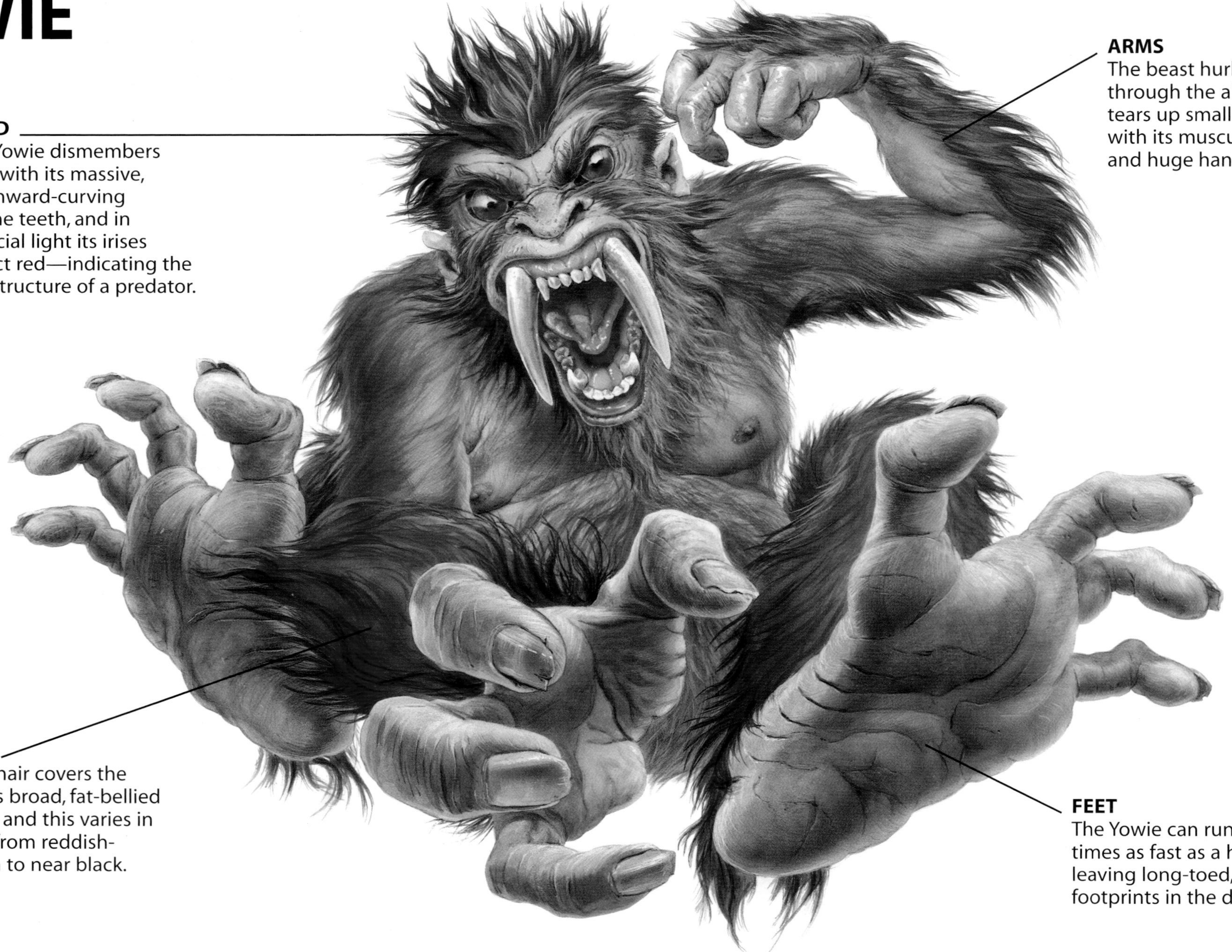

HEAD
The Yowie dismembers prey with its massive, downward-curving canine teeth, and in artificial light its irises reflect red—indicating the eye structure of a predator.

ARMS
The beast hurls rocks through the air and tears up small trees with its muscular arms and huge hands.

HAIR
Thick hair covers the beast's broad, fat-bellied frame, and this varies in color from reddish-brown to near black.

FEET
The Yowie can run three times as fast as a human, leaving long-toed, wide footprints in the dirt.

Huge, hairy and elusive, the Yowie allegedly hides out in some of Australia's most inaccessible regions. It hunts by night, stalking kangaroos and other animals through the bush before ripping off their heads. The Yowie can move at amazing speed over rough terrain—leaping over creeks and boulders. Occasionally, it wanders close to areas of human habitation, where it watches people from dense cover, and if disturbed, the Yowie stamps its feet, beats its chest and shakes trees until they snap. Sometimes, the creature charges at intruders: screaming and growling with ear-shattering intensity, displaying its long canine teeth, and releasing an odor of rotting flesh and bad eggs, so strong it can make you sick. Other people have been terrorized when the beast has attacked their vehicles or hurled rocks, while farmers have found the Yowie feasting on slaughtered cattle.

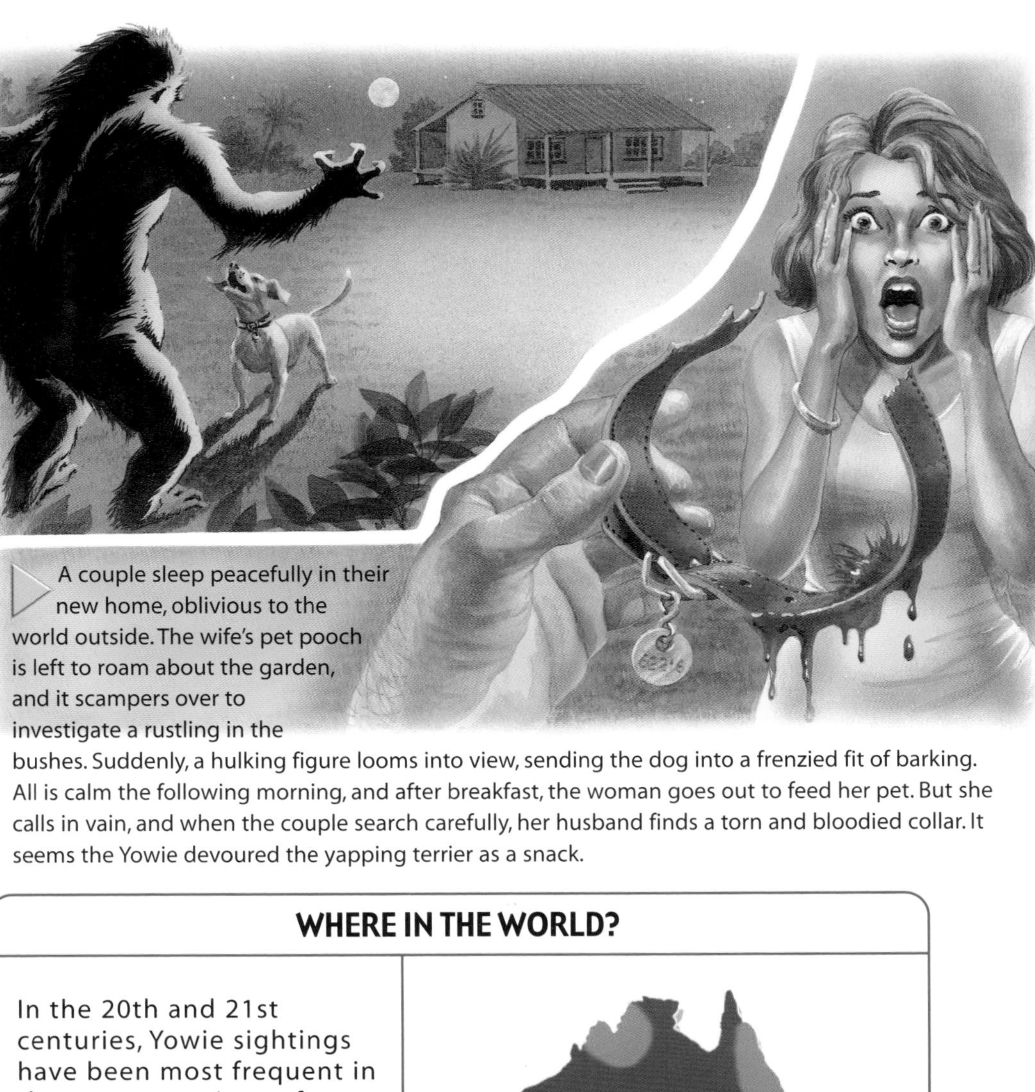

A couple sleep peacefully in their new home, oblivious to the world outside. The wife's pet pooch is left to roam about the garden, and it scampers over to investigate a rustling in the bushes. Suddenly, a hulking figure looms into view, sending the dog into a frenzied fit of barking. All is calm the following morning, and after breakfast, the woman goes out to feed her pet. But she calls in vain, and when the couple search carefully, her husband finds a torn and bloodied collar. It seems the Yowie devoured the yapping terrier as a snack.

WHERE IN THE WORLD?

In the 20th and 21st centuries, Yowie sightings have been most frequent in the eastern regions of Australia, particularly in the hills and forests of the Great Dividing Range that stretches from Queensland down to Victoria.

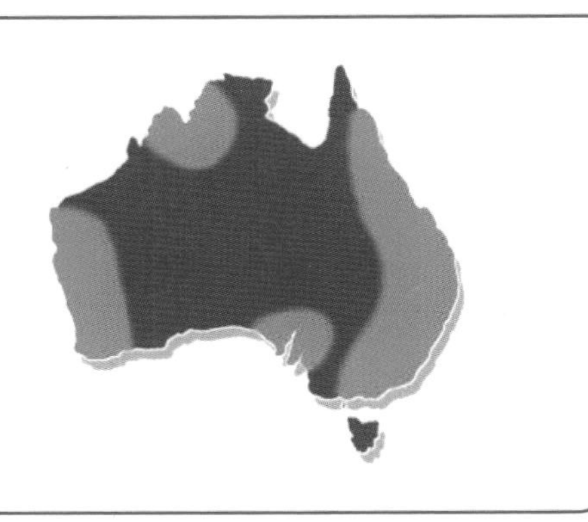

DID YOU KNOW?

- When a team of Royal Air Force surveyors landed by helicopter on a remote mountain peak in 1971, they found fresh Yowie tracks in the mud.
- In places where the creatures' prey has become scarce, people have seen Yowies scavenging on roadsides for animals killed by passing traffic.
- Yowies are immensely strong, and one startled individual even managed to overturn a moving jeep.

INDEX